THE HOTEL TITO

THE HOTEL TITO
IVANA BODROŽIĆ

a novel

translated by
ELLEN ELIAS-BURSAĆ

seven stories press
new york • oakland

Seven Stories Press
140 Watts Street
New York, NY 10013
sevenstories.com

College professors and high school and middle school teachers may order free examination copies of Seven Stories Press books. To order, visit www.sevenstories.com, or fax request on school letterhead to (212) 226-1411.

Library of Congress Cataloging-in-Publication Data

Names: Simić Bodrožić, Ivana, 1982- author. | Elias-Bursaâc, Ellen, translator.
Title: The Hotel Tito : a novel / Ivana Bodrozic ; translated by Ellen Elias-Bursac.
Other titles: Hotel Zagorje. English
Description: First English language edition. | New York : Seven Stories Press, 2017. | Translated into English from Croatian.
Identifiers: LCCN 2017031180| ISBN 9781609807955 (hardback) | ISBN 9781609807982 (e-book)
Subjects: LCSH: Women authors, Croatian--Fiction. | Yugoslav War, 1991-1995--Croatia--Fiction. | War victims--Croatia--Fiction. | BISAC: FICTION / Coming of Age. | FICTION / War & Military. | HISTORY / Europe / Eastern. | GSAFD: Autobiographical fiction. | War stories.
Classification: LCC PG1620.29.I44 H6813 2017 | DDC 891.8/236--dc23
LC record available at https://lccn.loc.gov/2017031180

Printed in the United States of America

9 8 7 6 5 4 3 2 1

CONTENTS

THE HOTEL TITO

I don't remember much of how it all began. I remember flashes: windows flung wide in our apartment, a stuffy summer afternoon, manic frogs from the Vuka. I wriggle between two armchairs and hum—*Whoever claims Serbia is small is lying*—Papa folds the paper and turns to me, I feel his irritation. "What's that you're singing?" he asks. "Oh, nothing, a song from Bora and Danijel." "Well stop it!" "You bet, ćale." "Don't call me ćale, I'm your papa, and damn *him* to hell!" I don't know why my papa's grumpy about the song or who *he* is, but I have a sneaking feeling it has to do with politics because everybody talks about politics all the time.

We're packing to go to the coast. For the first time ever my brother and I are going on our own. He's sixteen, I'm nine. Our neighbor Željka, a year younger than my brother, she's going too. I want to be exactly like her and I'm so thrilled because my mother and hers asked her to look after me. I don't sleep a wink all night. On the table between my brother's bed and mine are our passports. The light's been switched off and I ask my brother, can I come over to his bed? "Why passports if we're only going to the seashore?" I whisper. "Papa says if things heat up we'll go stay with Uncle in Germany," he says. I don't get the part about things heating but maybe this has to do with politics, too. I know a thing or two about politics myself, like I call my toy monkey Meso, because my monkey and our president look a lot alike. My brother and I try to imagine Uncle's life in

Germany. He says everybody there is so rich that apartments like ours would be for gypsies. I adore my uncle. He comes every summer, he has a young wife who's German, people listen when he says something and he smells super nice. This summer his wife brought along a little poodle, Gina, and Granny and Grandpa wouldn't have it in the house and they said it had to sleep in the shed. There was a huge fight, Granny said she'd poison the fleabag and Papa went to calm them down. Gina stayed in the house. Uncle brought us presents and marzipan, as always. I got a leather volleyball that couldn't be inflated. My brother got a soccer ball, but he never used it. Soon my brother chases me back to my bed and I spend hours that night thinking about everything.

The bus station in Vukovar smells, it's early in the morning, I'm sleepy and I'd rather be in bed. Papa's carrying me, even though I'm big, he carries me the whole way. He's wearing white pants and a blue T-shirt. We pull apart and kiss, first we make silly faces and then we air-kiss. It's our thing. There are lots of kids at the station and my brother and I take seats on one of the four buses. Our parents wave and wave, we wave, I can't see mine anymore but I wave to others I don't know and they wave back. They smile and call to us to take care, some kids' mothers cry. Some of them run after the bus to the corner.

◎ ◎ ◎

I've never been on an island before. We've been traveling so long I already threw up twice, and I'm not the only one. We even saw the sea a few times from the bus and then it went away behind a mountain. I'm sorry we won't have time to swim today, but I'm a little scared, too. We swim a lot at the Štrand beach by the river, but it's shallow there till you go very far out so knowing how to swim doesn't matter much. I only went to the Danube with my nana who said she swam like a stone, and while I watched the other kids in their inner tubes she only let me get my feet wet and splash my face.

When we finally arrived, I was put in a big room to share with twelve other girls my age. I'd already settled onto one of the beds when Željka came in with the head lady and said we couldn't be separated. That's how I ended up in a room with the big girls. I was happy and nervous. Some of them were grumpy about me being stuck in their room because they thought I'd probably spy on them and snitch to the head lady, but we all became friends pretty quick. I didn't talk much or bug them and I was polite to everybody. They called me "kid," and I was mesmerized by their spaghetti straps, deodorants, eyeliners, Tajči hairdos. Every evening out on the terrace at the resort we called Villa Drafty we had a disco. I kept being followed around by a boy, everybody said I should dance with him because he was the son of a famous actress. During the day we played Parcheesi and splashed around in the water. One afternoon my brother asked me to take a walk with him along the waterfront and when we got to the end of the pier he shoved me into the sea. I flailed around with my arms and screamed, the water was in my mouth, and he just stood there on the pier, shouting, "Swim, swim!" I don't know how, but soon there I was on the beach. I burst into tears, my clothes were soaked, and one of my white patent-leather shoes was gone. My brother said: "See, you're fine."

That's how I started swimming.

◎ ◎ ◎

We're already two weeks longer at the seashore than we were supposed to be. A few days ago we were on a bus ready to leave when they brought us back. We're unpacking our bags again. My brother stands over the sink and washes out our underpants and undershirts. Almost every day we're served fried fish for lunch and we're really starting to miss home. We go to the store for bologna sandwiches and yogurt. Now I'm sorry I left my newest Barbie, the one with the bendable rubber legs, at home because I was afraid someone might steal her, I only brought the plastic ones.

One morning when I went outside I saw Mama. I've never been so happy. She took us out for four scoops of ice cream each, and took me to a hair salon for an Italian haircut. They put her and Željka's mother in a special room in the attic, and I slept with her that night. I listened to them talking about a person walking through cornfields, about Mira who was nine months pregnant riding a bike, and a train where all the curtains were drawn, but in bed with her was cozy. I knew she'd argued with Papa, my brother told me. He didn't want to drive even as far as Vinkovci because somebody might think he was running away, and afterward, that same somebody might point a finger at us. I asked nothing about Papa so she wouldn't feel bad, but I did want to know when he'd be coming.

We've been on the seashore for a month now, the new school year is beginning and we have to go to school somewhere till we can go home.

◎ ◎ ◎

My uncle was there when we arrived at the Zagreb train station. We drove through the city. It was gleaming in the autumn sun. Our uncle's house was way out of town, I thought it was outside of Zagreb, but then I found out all of this is Zagreb. It's very big. They lived in a small two-bedroom apartment on the ground level and put us up on the next floor, which was empty. I often slept in my cousin's room, except when we fought. At first it was super nice there. Everybody treated me and my brother like we were special, and at the new school I had almost nothing to do but still got straight As. One afternoon my cousin and I were on our way back from school and when we were walking up the gravel path toward the house a siren began to wail. It was an air raid and I burst out screaming and crying. We raced into a neighbor's house. Nothing happened but it was the start of something new. Everything got trickier in the house. Once when I wanted to go into the bathroom, my older cousin blocked my way and said: "This is my house, I go first." The next morning while we were at breakfast, my mother's sister said to Mama, "You'll eat up all our bread." At first they were always baking cakes, but then there was less to go around, and we never opened the refrigerator ourselves. Sometimes when we went to bed we heard them talking in the kitchen. Papa usually called every third day, but then eight days went by and we didn't hear from him. On Saturday mornings we'd meet up in the main square with Željka and her mom. We'd hug and kiss like we hadn't seen each other for ages. The two of them were staying with relatives, too, and my father and Željka's were together back in Vukovar. We talked about what it would be like when we returned home. We went for *burek* or ice cream. On our way back we were quiet.

At first the people in Zagreb were better. They dressed better, they walked around on the wide streets and in the big squares, rode on the trams, without looking like they were doing anything special. They had toasters and dishwashers, there were cobwebs in the corner. That's how we saw them. Soon we, too, were riding around on the trams for free with a special yellow ticket and getting to know city tram lines. I could ride around all day long and eat nothing but salty rolls because we were always having to visit municipal offices, the Red Cross, Caritas for food supplies, that was fun. Once at Caritas we were given a big bag of sweets and were bringing it home to our neighborhood in Črnomerec on a tram packed with people. A dressed-up lady in our car said to her friend that the refugees are the ones crowding the trams because they're always out riding around day and night. I looked at her and smiled because I knew we were displaced persons, the ones from Bosnia were the refugees.

After two or three months of living in Zagreb some things became familiar. Autumn came and the rains started. Little by little the fun stopped. By then we'd spent nearly all the 300 Deutsch marks Mama'd brought with her. Fewer people were getting out of Vukovar and bringing us news about the old folks. That's what we called Papa's parents. Then one day we heard they had been killed. Throats slit. I heard the words distinctly. I was crouching behind the electric heater between the hallway and the kitchen. I think the grown-ups knew I was there, but they pretended not to see me and I pretended not to listen. They all became super kind to one another again, and I forgot all that. Mama was going into the bathroom more often and coming out with her eyes puffy. Papa hadn't called for a while. At that point my cousin and I began praying to God. We'd kneel in front of the sofa and pray so everybody could hear us, for everything we could possibly think of. For peace, for the Croatian guard fighters, for Petrinje, for Caesar and Cleopatra, and then we'd get all silly and giggly, but so no one could see. The grown-ups praised us for it and I told everybody I'd grow up to be a nun. We even pretended we were holding Mass and during one of our Masses the postman came to the door. He'd brought a letter from my father. Papa wrote he was well and wasn't hurt, he really missed us, we'd be seeing each other soon. The grown-ups thought this was a good sign and if anybody was going to save them from this hell it would be us kids. We were proud. A few days later I started noticing Luka and he was my first crush, he was a grade ahead of me. I gave up on being a nun but I still prayed to God for a long time.

◦ ◦ ◦

I came back from school in the afternoon. Mama was sitting in the dark, curled up on a kitchen chair. On the evening news they weren't saying a word but after the weather report they played the sad song "Moja Ružo." She knew the day had come, the Slovenes had announced the news over teletext, but our TV stations were saying nothing, they probably didn't know what to say. It's all over, whoever broke through is out, what will happen to the rest God only knows. My aunt came over and hugged Mama, she told her it's not true, they're lying, the Slovenes are as bad as the Serbs. Vukovar has fallen and this is bugging me because I'm not sure what it means exactly, and I feel stupid asking. Mama sends me to bed but they stay up for a long time. Early in the morning the phone wakes us. "I'm alive, I'm fine, see you soon." That's all.

Not where he's calling from, not when we'll see him, only that. We dance around the bed, hug each other, kiss.

My brother and I didn't go to school that day. We got everything ready and with Mama we went into town. With the money we had left we bought meat and all kinds of cakes. Mama and my aunt cleaned the house all afternoon, and in the evening we began to wait. I read the coffee grounds from a few cups of coffee and ran to the window whenever I heard a car. Midnight passed, but no one was sending us to bed. We guessed he was in Vinkovci, there must be crowds and chaos, and maybe they had to be inspected, organized, transportation found, whatever. After a while the three of us went upstairs and Mama placed a candle in the window and stayed up. The next day we went to school. With me in class was Lidija, her dad had broken through the day before. She told me mine was probably a prisoner now and I asked the teacher to let me sit somewhere else.

◎ ◎ ◎

Under the Christmas tree I got the jeans with knee patches I'd wanted most. My brother got a notebook with a Croatian flag and a cloth backpack for school. It was super cool and I think he liked it because he'd been carrying his books in our aunt's old briefcase. I wanted to give Mama something but I didn't have any pocket money. I came up with the idea of slipping a pack of cigarettes out of her carton of Benstons and wrapping it in colored paper along with a pack of Animal Kingdom chewing gum. My cousin got outfits for her Barbie and all of us were pretty happy with the gifts. There was lots of snow that winter and we went sledding. Soon it was time to start the second term, and I was still going to the same school, though I was certain I'd be back in Vukovar before the end of the school year. One evening my uncle came home and told my mother there was an empty apartment in New Zagreb. All we had to do was break in. He had a relative who'd jimmy the lock. Then they'd leave and Mama could wait for the police. No one would send a woman with two kids out into the street from an empty apartment, and if they did throw us out, at least they'd find us another place to stay. That was the most he and my aunt could do for us right now. Željka and her mother also left where they'd been staying with relatives and were put up at an army barracks in Pula by the sea. We talked once over the phone and cried.

◎ ◎ ◎

I'd never been on the fifteenth floor of a building before. The night before we moved into the apartment, I went out to Samobor to stay there for the night with Granny and her brother. Granny had escaped, after all, through Novi Sad and Hungary, it was only Grandpa whose throat was slit. For a time she stayed in a cellar with her neighbor Marica whom the Serbs had raped and shot in the eye. Nothing happened to Granny. The two of them lived on raw eggs and brandy. Then, somehow, Granny got away and later Marica did, too. She kept talking about it and she was telling everyone her son had probably been killed. No one wanted to hear that. In their house, on the hall table by the phone, there was this photograph of my father, brother, uncle, and Grandpa, and when they broke into the house, one of the Serbs picked up the picture and said he'd hunt them all down. Granny brought me from Samobor to the apartment and moved right in with us. My mother let us into the high-rise. She was tired and smiling. The apartment had two bedrooms, and the last person to stay there had been a Serbian woman from Derventa. She'd been subletting and we hadn't known about her because the apartment was being rented off the books. The woman was gone, but she gave my mother gray hair because she left an egg in the fridge, and when Mama entered the apartment the first thing she did was open the refrigerator. She was nearly scared to death that somebody was living there after all. The owner had been given the apartment by his job but he was scared of heights so he'd never lived there. He took us to court anyway to have us evicted. In the lawsuit he said he and his family had gone off on a trip over Christmas and when they came back they'd found us squatting. He said there was a danger of theft of personal belongings and damage to furniture. At court we were represented for free by a famous lawyer and in the papers there was even an article, "Law Written by Tears," about us. I read it so many times I knew it by heart.

The eviction notice recently served on a Vukovar family squatting in an apartment in a New Zagreb high-rise will be read by many as disrespect for the law. Finally, they'll say, after all these months while we've shrugged, helpless, watching daily break-ins justified by military uniforms, time as prisoners of war, or refugee status . . . But before we went to visit the Vukovar family we discovered that respecting the law differs from case to case. All the fates of these newest squatters are not the same. This story about how they moved in isn't so different from the others—it started when word got out of an empty apartment and three brave souls jimmied the lock, and it ended with the arrival of the police. This well-oiled routine ended this time, however, with an eviction notice and a summons to court in record time. And something else unusual in the case of this Vukovar family—the total negligence shown by the leaseholder who, as the neighbors and the folk from Vukovar tell us, never even appeared at the door to his place. He was in the building, apparently, but didn't stop in to visit his new tenants.

A PHANTOM LANDLORD: In conversation with the neighbors we learned they hadn't seen the negligent landlord in seven years, which is how long ago he was deeded the apartment by his company. Three years ago, when there was a thunderstorm in Zagreb and some of the windows were smashed, the apartment became a dovecote and breeding ground for disease! But not even then did the owner show up. The pigeons died and the filth was cleaned by an elderly gentleman, possibly the father. The two-bedroom apartment had a subletter who was not, apparently, liked by the residents: even though she lived there for three years the apartment was listed as empty. For, the Vukovar family says, we'd never have moved in if we'd known she was staying here. It just so happened that the apartment in dispute was visited that day by a three-member commission from the company that owned it in order to establish who was living there, since the time to condominiumize had come. Faced with the tears of the Vukovar family and their fate, the company committee relented, but the tenants couldn't remain there illegally—they had to have some sort of certificate for temporary use. The company allowed the Vukovar family to stay on until they found a new place to live. One of the commissioners even told them: "I'd sooner have you stay at my house than throw you out . . ." As many in the category of "wartime squatters" have been coveting apartments in the big city, it's clear that this family could only be there temporarily, until the institutions responsible for handling the problems facing displaced persons see to their needs. Until then, the company committee agrees that these people cannot be on the streets. The tragedy of this family with two children began with the fall of Vukovar. They've heard nothing ever since from their father. He stayed on to defend the city until the Chetniks and Yugo Army marched in, and then all trace of him vanished. He is not on the list of wounded or killed, he is not in the register of the International Red Cross who made the rounds of all the Serbian camps... The only hope left is that their father may be alive in one of the improvised camps in Serbia, out of bounds for the International Red Cross. Their property (two family homes and an apartment) they can live without one way or another, they say, but in Vukovar their grandfather's throat was slit. "We don't want someone else's property, we want to go back to what's ours even if it is in ruins. Please allow us a roof over our heads and compassion. We have to stay here though we'd rather be going home tomorrow," says the thirty-year-old mother in tears. "My son crosses the street without even looking at the traffic light. He says, 'Who cares.'"

○ ○ ○

At first we used only one room and the kitchen. In the other, bigger room were the things belonging to the woman who'd left. Mama said we mustn't touch anything. On the heap there were a fur coat, flashy scarves, baubles, boots, and a red handbag. The heap stood there in the middle of the room until the day Željka and her mother moved in, when we pushed it aside and covered it with plastic sheeting. At the army barracks where they'd spent a few weeks, they'd been sharing one bathroom with fifty people, and there were at least fifty with them in the room; they all slept on cast-iron double-decker beds. They couldn't stand it there so now there were six of us. I was super glad they were with us, it was cheerier. I think only Granny felt a little grumpy about it, but she did get her own room. The rest of us slept all together on the floor, on comforters and blankets. In the apartment across the hall from us lived Auntie Barica who'd look after me when the others went off to the prisoner exchanges. She made me crepes with tomato marmalade and took me to Bundek Lake, into the Sljeme hills, and to visit her sister out in Šestine. She never married and never had kids of her own so she really loved me. The apartment next to ours belonged to Uncle Rudi and Auntie Nina. They brought us poppy seed strudel and Auntie Nina would bring along her pendulum to tell us whether there was news about Papa. The pendulum always said he's alive, he's not in the ground, and he's healthy. Auntie gave Mama phone numbers of seers and numerologists who said the same. Just one man, who came out through a prisoner exchange, told Mama he'd covered my father with a sheet.

◎ ◎ ◎

Spring came to the park by the high-rise and I spent hours on a bench. I joined the public library and read three books a week. I read in the park, in the bathroom, on the balcony, during recess. I read everything I could get my hands on, I'd discovered a parallel world and moved almost totally into it. I woke up before everybody else, while the house was quiet, and raced out the door after drinking a glass of powdered milk. My mother and Željka's began working at Astra for minimum wage and left the house early. In the afternoon they'd go to Caritas sometimes to pick up food supplies or to the Zagreb Vukovar offices for any news. Around then the government began granting military rank to the people who'd stayed in Vukovar, and based on that they'd receive an army salary. We went to ask about my father, but nobody knew because he wasn't registered anywhere, yet he hadn't been killed. The computer listed him as part of Civil Defense and with that document they sent us home. This sounded fine to me, but Mama was angry and she kept saying: "He wasn't willing to drive his very own wife out of the city for fear they'd think he was running away, and now he's being labeled Civil Defense like the little old ladies cowering in their cellars." I didn't know little old ladies were in Civil Defense too. The next day we went back and Mama said she wouldn't accept the paper and to let somebody who'd really been there tell her what my father was doing, because she knew he'd bought a gun with his own savings. "He cared only about himself and wore a fanny pack," muttered a rude man in fatigues. Later I found out the man was Lidija's dad who'd made it out in the breakout. My mother began to cry and asked them to let her see a general. Later it turned out everybody knew my father had stayed to the end and that the rude man in fatigues was the one who'd left earlier. We waited for the general for a long time, but when he came, he was super kind and offered Mama coffee. He apologized and asked what we needed. Mama explained it all to him and right away he gave us a document that said Papa was a member of the Croatian army. "Do you need an apartment, ma'am?" he asked my mother kindly. "No, we have a place, all I needed was the certificate," she answered. We left happy. Papa was a defender, the only thing we didn't get was money, he hadn't been killed, he was missing. Out we went for ice cream.

◎ ◎ ◎

My brother and I never got along well. He'd make me eat hot dogs when he knew I hated them, and when he was looking after me I had to check in by buzzing the intercom every few minutes from outside. The game we played a lot was called "Border." He'd ask me: "Which country do you want to be, Yugoslavia or Germany? And remember Yugoslavia is where you're from and the Partisans beat the Germans." "Yugoslavia, I want to be Yugoslavia!" I'd shout. I had to cut up four little slips of paper, while all he needed was one because the Deutsch mark was worth so much more than Yugoslav dinars. Also my vehicle was one plastic truck from a gumball machine, while he had cars with batteries because Germany was so much more advanced. Pretty soon he'd confiscate even my one truck at customs because I didn't have the proper papers. I'd be on foot with the pedestrians, my Barbies, who weren't allowed to walk across the border. Then the game would be over because I'd wail, and he'd tell Mama: "We were just playing."

My brother started high school. He'd wanted to go to the commercial high school, but Papa had signed him up for the gymnasium, the most challenging school, and they fought about it something awful. I cried, I felt bad for him. I always cried when he was in trouble, but when I was in trouble he'd tease me. And besides, I could never tell when he was being honest. For a while I fell for his story about how he, Mama, and Papa, before I was born, lived in a castle in Germany and raised horses. When I was born they ran out of money so they moved to Yugoslavia. Because of this I both adored and hated him, he was big and smart while, compared to him, I was dense. Once, in second grade, I got a D. He predicted I'd finish that year with a B, third grade with a C, fourth grade with a D, and I'd flunk out of fifth grade, and my husband and I'd end up living in a musty cellar with only one light bulb. When we came to Zagreb he went everywhere with Mama. To the nighttime prisoner exchanges, and even to parliament where he argued with politicians. Mama let him do anything he wanted—stay up late, sit with the grown-ups while they were talking—anything except enlist. At his new school he ran into old Vukovar buddies; back home he used to sneak off with them to the barricades without our parents knowing. To go to Vukovar, this was their new plan. Luckily they weren't eighteen yet so nobody would let them. We hadn't heard from Uncle for ages. He probably didn't know where we were, and we didn't have the money to call Germany. One day Granny told us he'd been in touch with other relatives and he'd be in Zagreb the next day. My brother and I were crazy happy. And Granny was glad, too, but she was sad he'd see us in this sorry state, he was suffering over his brother's fate, it was worst for him. I felt bad. My brother and I didn't sleep all night. We believed Uncle would visit and we felt certain that when the school year ended he'd have us up to Germany over summer vacation. We started waiting first thing in the morning and Mama baked cakes. He arrived late in the afternoon and was a little miffed about the power outage and walking up to the fifteenth floor. He brought with him a bag of old clothes for my brother, and for me he brought colorful animal-shaped stickers for my notebooks. I was sorry to use them so I saved them until they started curling, and then I tossed them. He drank coffee and told us all this had made him quit smoking. He was in a big hurry because he was driving a truck and passing through.

I kept nosing around, aiming to slip into his lap. He picked me up and said, "What's up, little one, hard at work in school?" I announced, "Straight As at the end of the term and I'm competing in a contest for Croatian." He smelled so good and reminded me of Papa. My brother told him how he'd gone with Mama to parliament and how he'd told them that if they didn't resolve our situation he'd bring a mattress and sleep there. Uncle laughed like this was a huge joke, so we laughed too. Soon he put me down, even though I wanted to snuggle more, and from the leather bag he wore over his shoulder he took out an electric shaver. He showed us how it didn't even have to be plugged in. He switched it on so we could see how it worked and began to shave right there. Granny leaned over, and with a quick gasp asked, "Does that hurt, son?" but he only pushed away her hand and said, "Hey, old girl." From his wallet he took a picture of our little cousin we'd never even seen and said we could keep it. Time to go. Granny started crying, and he told her, "Hey, old girl, this is a nice enough place." We saw him to the door, and when we came back in Mama told us, "He'll have you up this summer for sure." Afterward I heard her saying to Željka's mother, "I never expected much from him anyway." My brother said nothing and scribbled away in his diary. I followed him into the room. "Why didn't he invite us?" I asked. "Because he isn't home now either, he's driving humanitarian aid around Croatia. He's doing the same thing Papa's doing," he answered. "We'll go to Germany this summer for sure," I parroted. "Beat it!" he said for no reason. "I didn't expect much from you anyway," I snapped and left.

◎ ◎ ◎

It was early morning and I was lying there awake in bed on the floor when I thought I heard familiar voices in the kitchen. There was nobody around me, which meant everybody else was up already even though it was a Saturday and there was no school. I thought maybe I was still dreaming. I went to the door and put my ear to it to hear better. Now I knew. Into the kitchen I flew and there were my nana and granddad, Mama's folks. We'd thought they were dead, the city had fallen five months before and we hadn't heard from them. They started crying, Granddad took me in his lap, and Nana could barely move because her upper body was wrapped in a plaster cast. It turned out that in their Vukovar neighborhood the Chetniks were a little better and didn't kill every last person, they just made them sign away their house. Then they were evicted, and somewhere along the way Nana broke her arm. We were overjoyed they were alive and now there were eight of us. Nana and Granddad joined Granny, Papa's mother, in her room. They were given the sofa bed because there were two of them, and Granny slept on two armchairs tied together. All of us who'd made it out alive were together now and that was nice. The only thing was that other problems cropped up because there was less money but more mouths to feed. And besides, my nana and granddad didn't get along well with Granny. Granny felt she had more right to be there, we were only allowed to stay because of my father, her son, while Mama's parents felt the same because we were being supported, after all, by Mama, their daughter. And other things pitted them against each other. At five one morning we were woken by shouts from their room. Mama ran in and saw Granny throwing her slipper at Granddad. She shouted he was a damned Partisan who'd blown up bridges. It was true that Granddad had been in the Partisans as a kid, when he was twelve the Partisans came to his village before anybody else and took him with them. I didn't believe he'd blown up bridges, I thought Granny made that up, I was ten, and I couldn't imagine doing such a thing. Home guardsmen were the first to come into my other grandfather's village, the one whose throat was slit, so my two grandfathers ended up on opposing sides. This almost pushed Mama over the edge and she said she'd toss them off the fifteenth floor, them and all the rest of us, if they didn't start behaving like normal people. I could see us flying. A pipe burst that morning in the bathroom and flooded part of the apartment. My mother and Željka's didn't go to work, they'd had it and they went off to a café instead. For a short time we received aid, then Mama got a new job. She came to pick me up at school, smiling for the first time in ages with good news. "Who gave you the job?" I asked. "Uncle Grgo, I'll work twice a week at his office, cleaning after the work day is over, and the salary will be more than I was paid at Astra. He even said you could come along and choose a pair of shoes," she said. I was thrilled because I had had to put up with wearing things I didn't like much, except for light-blue tights we'd bought on sale.

Uncle Grgo was Papa's childhood friend and his folks moved to Vukovar when he was little. He was super smart, he went to the university and put his little sister through school. He had a wife and two boys, and then they got divorced so he moved to Zagreb a few years before the war. He ran a company importing shoes. When I was very small Mama told me that once when I was at their house I picked up a large green bag and carried it all day slung over my shoulder. When we were leaving to go home I didn't want to give it back so Uncle Grgo gave it to me.

Since then he and I had been buddies. Of all of Papa's friends who came to Zagreb he was the only one who was really glad when we got in touch. Nobody else had the time. In the main square we'd run into Uncle Ivan, who stood there all day calling out in a creepy voice, "Foreign currency, foreign currency." I didn't understand what that meant, but sometimes he invited us for coffee, which Mama always declined, but once I said I'd like pizza so he bought me a slice. Another time he wanted to buy Mama roasted chestnuts, but she said no to that, too. The third and last time I saw him was when he came to our apartment in New Zagreb. He was carrying a metal box and Mama was surprised to see him. He came because he'd heard that Mama had broken into our apartment and he'd heard of another one that was empty not too far from there, so he wanted to ask her to go with him. Mama just looked at him like somebody had kicked her in the gut, and Granny shouted, "You have your own wife to take with you, leave my daughter-in-law alone." Mama saw him out and slammed the door. When she came back and sat at the table, I could see she was shaking. That spring I got to know the Kvaternik Square part of town because often, whenever I had school in the morning shift, I'd go with Mama to her job in the afternoon. Mama would do the cleaning after everybody had left the office, Uncle Grgo would always be waiting for us, he'd make Mama coffee, and pour himself a whiskey. Then they'd talk about my father. He always said how Papa was a good man, my mother made him who he was, and Papa loved her more than he loved his own brother. Mama was sometimes in a rush to clean everything as quick as possible and he'd sit there with his head in his hands reading papers. In the end he'd sigh and say, "I should've been there." Each season we were given new shoes and Mama got a Christmas bonus. Then we went shopping like everybody else for the holidays.

⊙ ⊙ ⊙

We'd take the no. 6 tram into the town center. The tram stop wasn't far from our high-rise, but the ride was pretty long so I never went to town alone, only with Mama, mostly when she went to work. I hung around the school and the neighborhood, trying to pick up the local way of talking without having to ask about words I didn't know and look stupid. Back home we didn't say *salty rolls*, we called them *long rolls*, and *hella* sounded lamer to me than *wicked*, which is what we said, their *dork* was our *moron*, and there were all sorts of other Zagreb words, some of them even different from one part of town to the next. They found my accent weird, and when I said my mother had picked me out new dungarees, instead of jeans, at Caritas, I was branded a hick and a refugee. In my New Zagreb class they were all super fashionable, they'd been studying English since they were six, changed clothes every day and had names like Lana and Borna. Among them I had no friends, but I did get to know a girl named Vesna in my neighborhood who was three years older and hung out with me every day. Later a brother and sister, Josip and Maria, moved there from Bosnia and their mother would invite me in every day for *burek* with meat. Vesna lived in an old corrugated-tin apartment building and I often sat on a bench near it. One day she sat down next to me and started talking. When we got to know each other she told me her Aunt Flo was visiting, and I said how great, terrific, but it was kind of strange that she'd be out in front of the building with me while her aunt was upstairs visiting. It was only two years later, when I felt something warm dripping between my legs during history class, that I found out I too had an Aunt Flo. Vesna was tall and skinny, she wasn't pretty exactly, but she had these beautiful long fingernails she did in red polish and she was always working on them. She was not a straight-A student, but she was friendly to all the kids, even the ones a lot younger. I never went to her apartment, where she lived with her mother who always worked the night shift, her father who'd stopped leaving the house and only watched soccer matches, and her brother Mladen who hung out at the stadium and scuffled with the kids from Trnje. They were true Zagreb locals. They hardly ever went anywhere over the summer, only occasionally to city-run vacation facilities. When Mama sent me to make a copy of Papa's picture for the Red Cross archive, Vesna took me to a photocopy place in the neighborhood. It cost a lot to make photocopies of color pictures, but we were hoping somebody might recognize him. Papa was grinning in the picture, he didn't look like himself, the shadow of the terrace roof out in front of Granny's house half hid his face. It had been the last summer we were all together, dinnertime when the first *kulen* sausages were on the grill. The lady asked me why I needed the pictures and, when I explained, she said her friend worked at the Wall of Love and gave me the lady's number. They were looking for missing persons and seeking aid for our country, they wanted to find out the truth, help kids with no parents, and moms. Sometimes they sent groups of kids for a vacation on the coast or even abroad to affluent families wanting to help kids hurt by the war. That was what I understood and I raced home with the phone number to tell Mama there was still hope, proud to be bearing the news.

◎ ◎ ◎

When we first arrived it was a beautiful day in early autumn. There were throngs of people, chaos, commotion. At the front desk of the old political school complex, otherwise known—by some of us—as the Hotel Tito, people were elbowing each other and squabbling. Everybody wanted a second room, or one on the first floor for the kids, or one for their husband who might come back, or some other privilege; they felt entitled to make a fuss. We stood to the side.

After we'd been squatting at the New Zagreb apartment for a few months the court gave us eight days to leave or we'd be evicted. We were offered a place to stay on the coast, but we preferred staying closer to Zagreb because otherwise everybody would forget us, and besides if Papa showed up he'd look for us there. Other people from Vukovar, who were staying at the Zagreb Holiday Inn, had heard about a nicer place in an area not far from Zagreb called Croatian Zagorje, so we went out there with them to have a look. I was super excited because Damir lived there now. I'd first seen him at the Holiday Inn back when he was still staying there. He'd been coming out of the elevator, super cute, and I'd fallen for him right away. My family and I stood near the front desk at the new place and waited to see what would happen. The loudest, who shoved forward as representatives of the headless, wailing mob, the ones with the largest families already settled on the second floor, started shouting: "Get lost, trespassers! Beat it!" They meant us and a few other families who'd come to see the new place, having fled the seaside barracks where there had been seventy people sleeping per room. I could hear women sobbing and I, too, began crying really loud. I knew somebody would notice, I didn't want them to throw us out and besides I was hoping I'd see Damir again. Suddenly this pretty woman in a uniform turned up, squeezed my shoulders and said no one would touch us and the loud-mouths wouldn't be the ones deciding who'd go and who'd stay, because there were plenty of rooms. I was proud I'd pulled that off so well. The loudmouth representatives grumbled, because they'd lost their chance to push the rest of us around, but in the end they relented. It was, after all, about women and kids who had nowhere else to go. I was super happy. We were given a room on the third floor, number 325, with three beds. A min-iature, sunny, cozy room with its own bathroom. Mama sat on a bed and began to cry. I couldn't understand, we'd gotten what we wanted, even though there'd been no guarantees. I went out into the hall. Damir was going into number 326 and said, "Hi." All night I couldn't sleep.

◦ ◦ ◦

The young and healthy were given rooms on the third floor, the ones who could manage all the flights of stairs. Two rooms down from us was Aunt Slavica with her two sons. Mario was soft-spoken and withdrawn, while Dejo was younger and more brash. When he walked by he'd grab the little girls by the butt or the tits we didn't have yet, he'd probably seen that somewhere. He wasn't very good at it because we'd duck and slip away, but after that he'd punch us hard in those same places and that hurt. All of us hated him, but at that point I began to grow like a weed and soon I'd outgrown him by a whole head and he left me alone. Aunt Slavica was always wearing these garish clashing

T-shirts and tight jean skirts and she was pretty bulgy. She had a frizzled perm and bright-red lips. She spent most of her time out in the hall with her neighbor Kaja, laughing loudly, sometimes even screaming with laughter. Some hated her because she was happy and because her time had come and she was still young enough to enjoy it. Her husband had beat her, they were poor and lived in a shack with no plumbing, and then he was killed. She was given his pension and bought a cassette player and sang at the top of her lungs by the open door. She never came into our room to ask how we were. In the room next to Dejo's lived my friend Marina with her mom and sister. Then they were given another room. That autumn was one of the last exchanges and her dad came back. We crouched all afternoon by her door waiting for her to come out and say what had happened. She came out with two big bags of candy when we were heading down to lunch. All pink and grinning she said her dad had showered for a whole hour to wash off the first layer of dirt. I asked her if he'd said anything about my father. It had slipped her mind to ask.

◎ ◎ ◎

We were among the last to move in so I didn't know anyone. At the front desk I saw kids my age. After two or three days in our room, I ventured out and started exploring the cold, dark halls. The rambling concrete complex was vast and easy to lose my way in. The dark, that's what I remember best, there weren't windows except in the rooms, and out of the dark would swim the faces of old people shuffling noiselessly among the catacombs. I skipped down the service stairs to the ground floor and at the end of the hall I spied a boy and girl. I started trailing after them, this was my fight for sheer survival in this vast new place. They seemed to be out exploring their new home and I meant to go along. They began glancing back and whispering. "Poor thing! Those socks! And your stork legs," said the little girl to me. I didn't answer. I stopped, then went on following them. The boy said: "Coming with us to steal bananas from the kitchen?" I said, "Okay."

They were my first friends. Biljana and Ivan. Bilja's parents were divorced. Her father was down by the coast and she was here with her mother. Her mother protected her from everything, both of them had been held at a prison camp. All the over-the-top worrying was what made Bilja so thin, frail, and see-through. Most of the time she was invisible, but at least everybody knew about her. I was glad she'd hang out with me. Later I forgot her.

Ivan also lived only with his mom, who hadn't been married to his dad. When his dad was killed, Ivan and his mom weren't given the pension. It went instead to his other family, the one he didn't live with. Ivan often slept on armchairs by the front desk. He stole ice cream, and then some of the grown-ups began paying him to steal tools and other things. He dropped out of school in sixth grade. I think I was a little in love even with him. He smoked a pack of Marlboros a day. His teeth started falling out and he turned yellow. He stayed short, but hung out only with the bigger boys. For them, just for the fun of it, he'd sometimes tie a cat to the bottom of a basketball hoop. When he and his mother were granted an apartment, people often spoke of her in the same breath as truck drivers and men from the ministries.

◎ ◎ ◎

In Conference Room Number Five they made a church. Mass was held there every Sunday. They built an altar on a big conference desk and covered it with a white sheet, and inside it were locked a hundred books about the party and framed pictures of Tito. At the end of the room there were three confessionals made of three pairs of back-to-back chairs. On Sundays we prayed to God and attended catechism classes there. Sometimes doctors came to give us check-ups in the assembly hall and talk to the youth about sex. A movie director came once looking for two kids to act in a movie. I signed up to try out for a role and I was so sure I'd get it. Fifty of us crowded around the big oval table. They were looking for actors between the ages of seven and twelve. To start with we stood up one by one and gave our first and last name and age. Then was the first round. I raced off to our room and told Mama we'd probably have to move back to Zagreb, then I went back. After a few minutes they read out the names of the kids going on to the next round. I missed my name and pushed through the boisterous crowd. When I reached the tall lady with the papers and said I thought they'd skipped me, she just looked over and said, "If we haven't called you, you can go." This was a shock, I couldn't believe I wasn't going on to the next round and wouldn't get the part. But nobody from the Political School did. In the end the movie was bad and everybody was disappointed. The main role went to the son of our former dentist. He didn't even know how to say his *r*'s.

◎ ◎ ◎

Granddad drank. Years ago, while he was young, he fell off a motorbike and cracked his head. Something was off after that and he started drinking. This was the official version. Sometimes less, sometimes more, but mostly he was on his feet and he'd find his way home. From those who'd stayed in Vukovar, we heard that he'd been riding drunk on his motorbike and had been shot in the ass with shrapnel. This was relayed with hoots of laughter. I heard only once that the Chetniks had plied him with brandy and he'd cozied up to them. If he'd had any schemes in mind, they had obviously failed because he signed his house away. I pretended I didn't know him sometimes. When I saw him heading my way, I'd spin around on the service stairs and flee. He always had a pack of little kids trailing behind him because he had pockets full of candy. He loved to play with them, but they were cruel to him. Until the day when Dražen's dad told Granddad he'd kill him if he saw him hanging out near his boy, sorry old lush. After that I kept my distance even more in the halls, but sometimes in the afternoon I went to their room. Granddad would be sleeping, but if he saw me he'd go all tender and give me a toy made of wire. He'd also give me pocket money and send me to the bar to fetch him a beer. I could keep the change. If only he'd shut his eyes for good that would be best for everyone.

I was loitering around the front desk once and ran into Ivan and Zoki. They said they were going to follow Granddad; every day he went behind the Political School at the same time, before dinner, and they were curious to see what he was up to, maybe he was hiding money or something. What was I to do? If he was up to something awful, it would be better not to see it, but I didn't want to abandon him. Off we went. We trailed some fifty feet behind, but Granddad didn't turn around. We went through the big grassy area behind the building and came to a little slope. There was a big bare rock sticking up out of the grass there and Granddad kneeled. We couldn't see what he was doing, and as Zoki wasn't scared of him, he went right over and said, "Granddad, where'd you hide the treasure?" Seconds later he came back. He said Granddad was crazy and was kneeling in front of a rock where somebody had drawn a cross in chalk. Still, I was relieved that he was just crazy, nothing worse, and back we went into the building in silence.

◎ ◎ ◎

Zoki was my age, he was always picking fights, spitting at other kids, and when you saw him you knew he was no good. His cousin told me that when Zoki was a baby his dad threw him naked into the snow in the yard when he wouldn't stop crying. His twin sister, Zorica, was in my class. On the last day of school, when we were on our way back to the Political School, Marina, Zorica, and I saw a mangy little kitten. We were thrilled. It was so small we could cup it in our hands, it had no fur in spots, but it was wiggling and softly meowing. We decided to save it. I pulled out the bag for my school slippers and put it in. We carried it to the hill behind the Political School, found a box and some clothes from Caritas, and wrapped it up. We agreed to steal a syringe from the infirmary and use it to feed the kitten milk. We'd take turns getting up before seven and bringing it breakfast. When it was Zorica's turn she overslept. We didn't say a word but we moved the kitten to a new place and began avoiding Zorica. One day when we were going out to the hill, we noticed her following so we turned and went back. Zorica came over and said, "I hope your dad never comes home." I spat at her but she dodged and ran off. I told everybody what she'd said and soon nobody would hang out with her. A few days later the kitten disappeared from the box. We searched the whole hillside but never saw it again. The summer went by and Zorica and I still hadn't made up. She was mostly by herself or with her cousin Nataša whom everybody called Dumbelina and who was borderline stupid. One afternoon I ran into Nataša and told her to tell Zorica I wanted to make up. Zorica came running over a few minutes later and from way off I could see she was smiling. She offered her hand and said she hadn't meant what she'd said. I didn't give her my hand. Instead I told her I was joking. I turned around and walked away.

⊙ ⊙ ⊙

Nataša had nicknames. Dumbelina, Poor Thing, and Beatles because her hair was like wire and her mother cut it like the Beatles'· nothing else worked. She pronounced it *Bitlus*, which made her sound even dumber. Her older sister Kristina had thick black waist-length hair, had graduated from the commercial high school, and was engaged to marry a local Zagorje guy. Their room was hospital pristine but still crammed with stuff. I know this because sometimes I went to Nataša's when there was nobody else around at the hotel. She called me every day and often tagged along because sometimes I'd be nice. When I went to her place, she'd show me everything she had, especially whatever she wasn't supposed to touch, like her sister's things. She took out Kristina's sanitary napkins once—pretending she didn't know what they were for—and said she'd give me one if I promised to come back the next day. Her father and mother lived in the next room, her mom was a quiet woman who spent her days tidying and cleaning, while he, in his own eyes, was this big-time Don Juan. Everyone knew he was up to something with the local Zagorje girl who worked the front desk.

I started a dance group and chose the girls to dance in it. I came up with the choreography and decided which songs we'd dance to and what we'd wear. For our rehearsals we were even allowed to use Conference Room Number Four, the one used every morning for daycare. When we'd rehearsed a number we'd paste posters around the front desk and invite people to come and watch us in the sports hall. It was mostly old folks and little kids who showed up by the stage, but we were sure they wanted to be just like us. Dumbelina followed us around all that time and wanted to dance in the group. We conferred and agreed—no way. We were working on a song that opened with a rapper rapping before the singer started singing and I thought we could use a boy to do the rapping while we danced, but we couldn't find a boy who'd agree to. The day before the perfor- mance there was some big commotion, a woman was shouting and I could hear gasping sobs. Dumbelina appeared beet red on the service stairs. I asked her what was up. "He took off with that Zagorje slut." I think the worst part for them was that the woman was a local from Zagorje. I told Nataša if she wanted to she could dress all in black and wear a baseball cap and come to the sports hall. She could stand next to us and be the rapper boy. She said she would, but the next day her mother didn't let her.

⊚ ⊚ ⊚

Conference Room Number Seven was the most popular spot in the whole Political School. The front desk had let the teen crowd use it for their New Year's party, Parcheesi sessions, card games, and general socializing. Everybody between thirteen and seventeen was there. I was a little younger but I knew what Number Seven looked like because I'd lurk on the service stairs that passed right by it and peer in every time the door was open a crack. All of us who hung out by the door to Number Seven peered in, and whenever anybody who was inside spotted us they'd slam the door in our faces and leave us in a cloud of smoke. There were a few armchairs in there, a sofa with stuffing spilling out in places where it had been gashed with a knife, and some stools. A Ping-Pong table stood in the middle. And nothing else. The walls were covered with Post-its in different colors with dumb things kids had said. Most were Dumbelina's bloopers, but she didn't go there often so they probably didn't upset her. My first foray into Number Seven was after the good doctor from Vukovar visited our accommodations; he distributed a carton of Marlboro Reds to every person at the hotel, and when I say every person, the cartons weren't given only to the adults but literally to every two-footed resident. A truck parked out in front of the hotel, they unloaded the cigarettes, and two men stood there with a list of the rooms and residents. I waited in line to collect our cartons. After half an hour I was given the three packages and went back into the hotel. I decided to tell Mama they'd given me cartons just for her and my brother. I knocked at Number Seven. There was no sound from inside so I sat on a bench and slid the cartons under my feet, just in case somebody I knew passed by. Soon, from the dark of the room, Miro poked out his head and said, "What's up? What do you want?" "I brought you smokes," I said softly. He grabbed the carton and banged the door shut. Behind me appeared Dragan, on his way in he asked, "What are you doing here?" "I brought you smokes," I said again. He laughed, baring his yellowed teeth. "Wanna come in? You know what they're up to?" he leered. I looked in over his shoulder but it was nearly dark so I could only see silhouettes on the sofa. I heard Miro's voice and a girl's. "What are you doing?" I asked. "Spin the bottle in the dark," said Miro. "Now get lost and come back at New Year's," said Dragan and shut the door.

I shouldn't have given them the cigarettes, I said to myself, mounting the stairs. I handed Mama the two cartons. "That's all they gave me," I said. "So they stiffed us for that, too, well, I guess I'll smoke less," she sighed. I was relieved she hadn't seen through my ruse so I sat in her lap and hugged her. After that Miro always said hi in the halls. My friends kept asking why and I pretended I had no clue. By New Year's I'd begun wearing a bra with no underwire and managed to sneak Marina and Jelena in with me to the party.

⊛ ⊙ ⊚

The infirmary was in Conference Room Number One. Our nurse, Ružica, worked there with Dr. Big Pig. The nurse let us play with plastic syringes, bandages, and leftover boxes. We hung around the improvised waiting room, which was actually in the front entrance hall next to the big stairs. Along the wall, across from the door, stood ten chairs that were all full when the infirmary was open. The waiting room was always crowded with old folks, and to the left of the crowd, by the door, was a spot where we played Chinese jump rope. There were dozens of places all over the Political School that were roomier and empty, but nobody would have been there for us to bug, and things were always happening here, like anywhere where people come for help, and needle each other, and squabble. This was where the action was. We knew we irritated them but we didn't care. Once we'd figured out who the regular patients were and who were the meanest, we were mean back. They became an everyday, essential part of our twisted little games. Old lady Pundjara lived alone, no family, not even distant relatives, and she visited the infirmary daily. Her only friend was old lady Milica who had diabetes and was a little quirky, and every time she walked by us she'd stop, lean on her elbows, and sing: "A cute young thing goes strolling by, her little chick is open wide, Granddad says tuck it, Grandma says fuck it." Then she'd cackle and walk on. She was a nutcase but she didn't hate us. Old lady Pundjara had a swollen, gnarled leg; her other leg was normal. She limped, but when she ran after one of us she'd scamper with amazing speed. If she caught whomever she was chasing, she'd crush the kid between her vast waist-length tits and between them was a smell so sickening your head would spin. We'd set our jump rope up right in front of her or tie it to the chair next to hers, and start hopping like elephants, as wild and loud as we could possibly be. After a few minutes old lady Pundjara would get up and try to yank away our elastic band, shouting furiously, "Beat it, vermin!" Once she managed to grab little Ivana's ponytail and yanked out a handful of her hair. After that we decided to take our revenge. We followed her and found which room she lived in. We multiplied the room number by 100 to get her phone number, and we crossed our fingers that she had a phone.

We chose Marina's room because she and her sister had it to themselves and dialed the number. "Hello?" said a hoarse voice. We said nothing. "Hello? Who's this?" said the voice. I took the receiver from Marina and blew into it, I'd seen this in the movies. "Motherfuckers, rats! Beat it, rotten pipsqueaks!" the receiver squawked so loudly that those standing farther away could hear. We were solemn. Nobody said a word, and then Marina hung up, picked up the receiver again, and dialed the number. We sat in silence, staring at one another. "Hello?" the same voice said. Jelena puffed into the phone. "Oh, you filthy creeps! God willing worms gorge on your gut, crabs drag you down the road, your own mother poisons you! Beat it, stinking vermin . . ." This time I was the one who hung up. We all were silent. The curses we'd heard scandalized us and we didn't want to listen to any more of them, but still, at the same time, this was all super thrilling. We didn't call her back that afternoon, but we gave her number to Zoki, Ivan, and the other boys. They liked it even more and thought this was a riot so they called her all the time, sometimes even at night. After that, whenever we ran into old lady Pundjara, we always said loud hellos and laughed. We didn't play Chinese jump rope right next to her anymore. And only sometimes, hardly ever, when we didn't have any other way to kill the boredom, we'd dial the number, set the receiver next to the phone face down, wait a minute or two, and hang up.

After a few years old lady Pundjara came down with cancer and died, so she never lived long enough to go back to Vukovar. They buried her in Zagorje, on the little hill, and she had no family of her own to take back her bones.

◎ ◎ ◎

A hundred of us enrolled in the village elementary school. Most of the kids were from the Political School and a few were Hilltoppers, our nickname for kids from Vukovar who were staying at another hotel on a hill. They'd been accommodated there before we arrived, their hotel was fancy and partly underground, and it had been used before the war for tourists and conferences. We joined forces in our war against the Piglets— our favorite nickname for the Zagorje locals—which began on our first day at school. The war was cruel and went on for ages, with the rare ceasefire and only sometimes real friendship. We were all about the same age, all equally poor, but our group had come from Vukovar, a city, a real urban center with a main square, baroque buildings, a café, and a Nobel Prize winner, while all they had was a pastry shop, Suljo's, and their mangy commie president Tito who made this whole mess in the first place. Our main arguments were rock-solid. And besides, they reeked of pigs, their boots were caked with mud to the knees, the kids in the upper grades came to school drunk, and there were pregnant Miss Piggies. A few of the Piglets were from a real village where there was a school and street lamps, but the rest were from scattered hamlets, too small to even have a name, so we dubbed them, collectively, Zagorje Village. The backwoods Piglets spoke in a language we couldn't understand, it sounded more like Albanian mixed with Slovenian. We called them basket cases. We and they received handouts, but they did so willingly, or were simply stupid and lazy, while we were stuck there because of the Serbs. We despised the Piglets and they despised us, and we clashed individually and in groups. To them we were trespassers, a threat, displaced persons with government subsidy and VCRs, living in a hotel where we were served meals; they'd have given one of their cows for a week of a life like ours. Meanwhile, we were clueless about whether a cow had horns, so they made fun of us. They couldn't imagine how little we cared.

With me in class were Dumbelina, Vesna from Vukovar—a Hilltopper who'd become my close friend—and Ivan, but he dropped out a year later, so it was just the three of us from our crew. At first we scoffed at the other kids, while maintaining diplomatic relations with the ones who kept cleaner and had better grades. There were a few we could understand, crib from on a test, fend off the loneliness with. As the years went by some became almost friends, but we were always us and they were them.

Most of them were your standard Zagorje Village issue. Brothers Ivek and Marijan walked three miles to a bus stop where they were picked up every morning at 6:00 a.m. and dropped off at 4:00 after the bus had made a big loop through the hills. Marijan kept up with Cs, he was quiet and had not a single front tooth. Ivek was a little slow, more so than our Dumbelina, yet he knew all the saints' days. This was all he knew. He sat with Zdenko who was horribly fat and stupid, and when we had a test for Croatian, two identical tests appeared with Zdenko's first and last name on both. The second was Ivek's. They both made it to the eighth grade. Žućko sat in the dunce's seat, he was small and bad. He came to school drunk because for breakfast he ate bread soaked in wine. He lived with his grandmother who told him this was what baby Jesus ate. Žućko, too, made it to eighth grade. In front of me sat Veronika who always stank of pigs, she had greasy hair and bulgy blue eyes. They all had the last names Antolić, Županić, or Broz. I'd hardly spoken to Veronika but then Granddad made friends somewhere with her dad, who liked to drink too, and he gave them things from Caritas that none of us wanted, like UN shampoo and toothpaste, and Veronika said they foamed up real nice and smelled good so she started being nice to me. We still didn't talk much because she was sure there was this city in America called Chicago, but she was always bugging us to come visit and see her baby bunnies. One spring afternoon we went.

She was living in a tiny house on a hill with countless snotty brothers and sisters who were all small and grimy. They had only two rooms, one where they cooked and ate, and the other where they slept. We had only one, but we decided they were worse off. The baby bunnies were behind the house in a wooden stall. As soon as we went in we were hit by a sour stench and it took us a minute to get used to the dark. On the floor was a cardboard box and in it were a few furry balls. "Here they are," said Veronika, in awe. "Wow, they're so tiny. Super sweet!" said Marina and I. Never in my life had I seen such tiny rabbits, I was entranced and felt it had been worth climbing up the hill. "Can I hold one?" I asked. "Mama doesn't let me, but you can, just be real careful," she answered. They were all adorable, most of them were sleeping, but they wiggled their little snouts in their sleep. I chose a white one. Once I'd seen my grandfather carry a rabbit by the ears. I grabbed it firmly and lifted it up. Something went crunch. "Not the ears! Not the ears!" screamed Veronika. I set it down fast but the little snout wasn't wiggling anymore. "Mama'll kill me, why'd you go do that for?" "I didn't do anything, I didn't even pick it up all the way," I started protesting. "Can't you see it's done for, you dummy!" she wailed. "You still like our shampoos, jerk!" said Marina because she, too, had given her some. "Let's go," I said to Marina and headed for the door. We were blinded by the sun and

Veronika's dad surprised us, standing in the doorway. "Hey there, city girls, are those bunny rabbits cute or what?" he leered with a toothless grin. We didn't answer, we hurried toward the gate. When we'd slipped through we ran down the hill. The next day in school Veronika and I didn't greet each other. She didn't talk to anybody, she kept flicking a lock of greasy hair over her left eye.

◎ ◎ ◎

The last class on Fridays was catechism. If we'd had a choice, we would have preferred even a math class, but we didn't, and we hadn't learned yet about skipping. We all had to attend; whoever loved Croatia was supposed to love God, too. Only Aida from the C group went home early. Reverend Juranić came into our classroom before the bell; as soon as it rang he'd start praying and it wasn't just the Our Father, like the other catechism teachers, but the Hail Mary, the Creed, and sometimes, if he was inspired, a circle of the Rosary. He'd flash his eyes at us one by one, walk around, lean over, and when he caught a kid mumbling he'd hush us all and the kid would soldier on alone. If the kid didn't know the words, he'd get an F or a knock on the head. Then the reverend would go to his seat in silence, and take out a juice box and straw and one or two chocolate bars, a Mars bar or a Snickers, from his black bag. We'd watch him eat and drink, our mouths watering. If he heard a word from somebody in one of the back rows, he'd heave a piece of chalk or whatever he could lay his hands on at them. He told us we were fools, idiots, lazy. None of us seriously thought we'd fail catechism, but the fear and uncertainty that Juranić, with God's help, radiated were so intense that we trembled before him. Sometimes he'd

take groups of students on trips to the Marija Bistrica shrine
and then, in rare high spirits, he'd pull one of the girls with long
braids onto his lap. Her cheeks would blaze red and all the way
home she'd stare at the floor. We felt he hated the Vukovar kids,
we weren't given special treatment but we were on our guard.
Toward us he was every bit as derisive as he was toward the
others, but he tailored his questions to us: "So tell me, Vukovar
kids, how does one clean a stable?" And then he'd say, "You're too
high and mighty, the village kids are closer to God. Jesus slept in
a stable, not a hotel," and he'd roar with laughter. Once he asked
Dragan, who was in eighth grade, about the Holy Trinity, and
when Dragan said, "Dunno," the reverend gave him an F. Then
Dragan asked, "Do you know what they call the Pope's cock?"
The reverend's face swelled and he reached for the class register
to bash the boy, but Dragan flew out from behind his desk and
flung himself at the reverend, shouting, "The Holy C, the Holy
C." The reverend bellowed and Dragan fled. He ended up at the
school psychologist's office, but nothing horrible happened. The
reverend scowled but no longer threw things at us.

As Christmas neared, we were asked to write an essay for
catechism homework about "My Christmas." The best essays
would be read at the school pageant. I believed in God and essay
writing was my favorite assignment. I had almost no competition in our class except a Piglet, Željka, who excelled in grammar
and whose sentences bristled with epithets. I made an effort to
write the best essay because with all my heart I wanted to read
it at the school pageant, I knew that would bring Mama out of
our room, and maybe for the occasion she might wear something dark blue instead of black. The reverend and the Croatian
teacher chose Željka and me. I was over the moon; before the

reading I was also performing a dance with my friend Ivana, we were presenting choreography I'd come up based on the song "Paloma Nera." I hadn't shown it to Mama because I wanted to surprise her, I was hoping this would be a big treat. She knew I could write well, but I thought I'd outdone myself this time. I changed from the sailor top and frayed hot pants I'd worn for the dance number into a white blouse and plaid pleated skirt and went out onto the stage for the second time. I was solemn, standing tall, and I waited until everybody was quiet and I had the total hush my essay deserved. I began to read. I breathed all my air into each sentence; soon I was breathing more shallowly and running short of breath. I hoped no one noticed that I was speaking more and more loudly until I was almost shouting the words and phrases that mattered most. All the highlights were here: a poignant pine branch, a missing father, Mama's widow's weeds, my brother who didn't have the change to buy a cola, and only one wish: home . . . When I finished, the people in the audience applauded, some wildly, others less so, the moms from the Political School dabbed at their eyes. Željka climbed right up, stood next to me, and began to read. I felt the audience would have liked to applaud me more but couldn't because she was already reading and they'd miss hearing her. Confused, I stood there, my head spinning, her words ringing: roast turkey with dumplings, midnight Mass, bracing fresh air, baby Jesus, gifts, dreams . . . When she finished she bowed so low to the audience that her long hair swept over her blushing cheeks. She was pretty. People rose to their feet and clapped like crazy. It was the end of the whole pageant so the applause was for all of us.

From the loudspeakers music rang out and the dance began. Students and parents were scattered across the hall and stage and there was no way I could spot my mother. I pushed with difficulty through the crowd of glowing faces, large and small, thinking she might have left. When I finally reached the exit I caught sight of her through the glass door where she was standing outside, smoking. She was wearing a big black coat with white epaulettes and her curls were full of fat snowflakes. I almost knocked her down when I flew over to throw my arms around her, shouting, "How did I do?!" "Where's your jacket? You'll catch your death!" she said, hugging me. "In the locker room, tell me, tell me," I pressed. I saw her chin wobble, like with kids when they start crying, and I was sorry. I realized I should have written about something else, I was stupid for not remembering the essay would make her sad. Like for her birthday two weeks before, when I'd given her a card with a picture of a king and queen and her eyes filled with tears, probably remembering Papa. From now on I'll write only for a good grade, I thought. I hung around her neck and said, "Don't cry, Mama, you know dear God disciplines those he loves most." She gave a strange little sigh and brushing away tears she said, "Uncle Grgo sent you a big bag of sweets." I was happy, I left the dance behind and went back with Mama to our cozy room. It was a nice Christmas Eve, we snuggled and watched good movies about Jesus, with the bag of candy by the bed. The only bad part was that I threw up and the next day my stomach hurt.

◎ ◎ ◎

Once we'd crossed the border we were given bag lunches and then for the first time I tasted iced tea which I'd never heard of before, it was disgusting but I had to drink something to keep from dehydrating and recover. At just after five in the morning, when my brother had come to see me off, I'd thrown up twice on the Zagreb city bus, before the real trip in the charter bus had even begun. I could have wept it was so embarrassing, but I pressed my lips together and stopped my chin from trembling, hoping I wouldn't cry because that would have been even worse. I clung to my brother who held, as far away as he could, the stinky bag and said for the third time that I never should've eaten bread soaked in milk for breakfast. This was the first time I was traveling on my own, and it was to a foreign country, to visit a family I'd never seen before and whose name I didn't even know, but for some reason they'd chosen me of all people to be their guest for two weeks. It was supposed to be fun, they'd take me to Gardaland, we'd go on daytrips, hang out together, and I'd forget all the bad things that had happened to me, while they'd pat themselves on the back about their good life. I was thrilled, I knew no Italian except the one word they taught us on the bus, *grazie*, probably assuming we'd need to say that the most. The closer we came, the more intense was the fever pitch of excitement. Jelena and I sat together and fingered the cards with the names of our families. Her parents were Mr. Gabrielle and Mrs. Nicola, and we were sure the names had been switched by mistake because we couldn't imagine a woman could be named Nikola. In my Italian family there were three kids, in Jelena's just one, so we thought mine would have more toys. The other kids on the bus weren't asleep anymore, some of them were boisterous and jumping around, I didn't know most of them because they were from other accommodations. There was one little girl who crouched silently, despondent, alone; I heard her mother and father had been killed and now all she had was her grandmother. She didn't even have a suitcase, just a plastic bag with six pairs of underpants. Vlatka told us about her, she knew her from Plava Laguna. The girl's name was Ana. Our hearts sank when we passed through the Mantua suburbs. Supposedly we were visiting well-to-do families, we were expecting villas with swimming pools like the ones in the *Beverly Hills, 90210* TV series, but what was rolling by us was totally different. Little houses in rows, all a strange shade of orange, and then buildings that weren't even high-rises, and wherever you looked there were tall smokestacks in the distance. Finally we came to *our* town, drove through the city gates and pulled up at the town hall where *our* families were waiting. It was a noisy crowd of grown-ups and kids waving at our bus. Some of them held big cardboard signs with names: Jelena, Marko, Sasha, others. The organizers left me with an older couple and a little boy, and I smiled at them and didn't understand anything. Just as I was beginning to wonder where the other two kids were, a little curly-haired girl appeared. She tweaked me by the card around my neck and called out: "Eccola qui, eccola qui!" She grabbed me by the hand and pulled me away. I didn't understand what was happening. There were two families fighting over me. I was starting to feel uncomfortable when a translator showed up and explained to the older couple that their little girl had stayed in Zagreb after coming down with something before the trip.

The curly-haired girl was thrilled that I was going with them and that she'd been the one to find me; in the car, on the way to their house, she held my hand and sat right next to me. They all kept turning to me, speaking in Italian and smiling, and I didn't understand a word. Then they'd repeat what they'd said, louder, enunciating more clearly, like I couldn't hear them properly, and I smiled and repeated, a little louder: "I do not understand." All I could grasp was that their son wasn't with us but he spoke English. The first thing I saw when they brought me into the house was a grand marble staircase and paintings on the walls and I thought they must be super rich. They took me to the second floor to the big bedroom I'd share with their daughters. They showed me an empty closet where I could stow all my things but what I had fit on just one shelf. They explained all this with their hands because their son wasn't home yet. The younger girl tagged along with me the whole time and when I went to the bathroom she waited by the door. When I came out, she pointed downstairs and brought her clenched fist to her mouth over and over, like Tarzan explaining to his girlfriend he'd made her dinner. I understood it was time to eat and down we went to a vast dining room with a long table and leather chairs.

More people I hadn't met were there and I kissed them and was introduced. Here was the seventeen-year-old boy who knew English, but he spoke it so strangely that it was tricky to catch what he was saying. I ate a full plate of pasta with spinach, they called it *pesto, pesto*, and when I couldn't eat another bite they were disappointed, so I said: "Good, good." They had to understand that. They looked me over and I knew they were talking about me so I felt shy. My head was spinning from the noise. Then the phone rang, the father answered and said to somebody: "Si, bambina jugoslava." After those words I didn't understand the rest, but this first part rang in my head and I felt the blood rush to my face. *Bambina jugoslava*, that's what he called me. No longer was I smiling shyly; I waited for the father to finish. When he came back to the table, I looked him squarely in the eye in the sternest way I knew, and said, "Croatia, no Jugoslava, bambina Croatia." That night I fell asleep with my face deep in the feather pillow, sobbing so no one could hear me and praying to God that the two weeks would pass quickly.

They bought new clothes, and not only for me, but for my brother and Mama. Whatever they offered me in the store I liked, and whatever I was given, Lettizia and Isabella were given, too. Marissa was my Italian mother. On her shoulders was draped the gaudiest orange-and-pink top with garish parrots. That's what she chose for my mother and I was ashamed to say no, my mother wore only black and dark blue; I hoped she might at least sleep in it. I was given two new bathing suits because it was summer and every afternoon we went to the city pool. The huge stores and shopping centers made me dizzy and I dreamed of the day I'd come back to the Hotel Tito with all these things and tell everybody what I'd seen. It was a thrill I couldn't share with the Italian family, they were so good to me, my whole face turned into a little smile that never quit. And they kept saying: "Cosa vuoi? Cosa vuoi?" By then I knew this meant *whatever you like*. And in the end I was given a big green suitcase because, of course, otherwise I'd never have been able to carry everything home. I look five times better, I thought, than if I'd gone to Germany. Just wait for Uncle to come and see me now. One afternoon we were supposed to attend a birthday party for a friend of Isabella's, and I heard there'd be another *bambina jugoslava* there, not from our bus but somebody who'd moved there two years before, so I'd have somebody to talk with in Croatian, though after the first few days, surrounded by Italian and with a little dictionary in my pocket, I'd begun understanding simple sentences and questions and was able to give an answer. On the way to the girl's house, in the car, Giorgio, my Italian father, began asking me about something in politics. He was usually super serious and almost never joked, different from my real father. That was how he spoke with his kids and with me. He mentioned Tito and Tudjman. I tried to be clear because obviously he didn't quite understand so I said, "Tudjman buono, Tito no." I repeated this again. He nodded pensively. Then he mentioned his own father, gestured with a wave behind him, like it was a long, long time ago, Zadar, ćevapčići, *ražnjići*, and he when he was *piccolo*. They must have been on a vacation in Croatia when he was little, I just nodded and repeated: "Zadar, bello." Later I learned that old Giuseppe, his father, was in Zadar, but Zadar wasn't Croatia but Italy, and his dad wasn't there on a vacation but to do with something I didn't quite catch. Soon we arrived, took the gifts out of the trunk, and went in to see the birthday girl. There were a dozen kids there. They were noisy and were playing party games in a half circle. When Isabella and I came in there was a hush and some of them pointed at us. I said ciao softly and sat down next to a boy. Mostly I didn't understand and assumed the girl I was supposed to talk with hadn't come yet because they were all speaking Italian. Suddenly one of them, looking at least fifteen, came over and said, "Hi, I'm Maja, I'm from Belgrade, and you?" She was pretty, she had long curly hair and dimples. I froze. "I'm from Vukovar," I choked. I couldn't look at her. "Great, so we can speak Yugoslav," said Maja. "I speak Croatian," I snapped. "Well it's all the same," smiled Maja. "It is not," I said and went off to the farthest corner where I found a chair. I sat there, shivering, longing for us to leave. Maja went back to her friends and prattled on in Italian. After half an hour, Isabella led me back to them. They explained something but I didn't understand and didn't even try. Maja no longer looked my way. An Italian girl stared at me and she rolled her eyes a little when she said to Isabella: "É noiosa." On the way home I checked the dictionary to see what *noioso* meant. Boring.

◎ ◎ ◎

The two weeks passed quickly and I was already understanding Italian better. With the help of the person leading our group I learned that my Italian family wanted me to visit them again. They invited me to stay at their house in Sardinia for the month of August. They really liked me and I'd begun to like them so I said I would if my mother would let me, though I was a little scared and I'd never been separated from my family for that long. They'd pay for my plane ticket and take care of everything, the only thing they needed from my mother was her permission. Why not, but it was so far off that it didn't seem important; what mattered was that by this time the next day I was going to be in our cozy room. That evening they were taking me to a restaurant, they'd given me a special dress lined with lace to wear, and after that I'd sleep through the night and then my family would be together again. I thought the other kids in our group would be at the dinner with their families, but it was only us and some people we didn't know. I'd been with Papa to eat at his hotel, we always went on the last day of school when I brought home my certificate with an "excellent" mark for comportment, and Papa'd order me a hamburger and three scoops of ice cream.

There was no way I could explain what I wanted to eat so I let them order for me. In general I wasn't thrilled with Italian cooking, they always ate pasta first, and sprinkled everything with this cheese that tasted the same way the apartment smelled where Granny Djuka, our Vukovar neighbor, lived, and she had four cats. They poured olive oil that was green over everything and it gave it all the same flavor. After a while the waiter came and brought me a few thin slices of prosciutto and two slices of cantaloupe, all on the same plate. I'd been hoping that this place would be a little nicer than my father's restaurant at the Hotel Danube, but I saw we were way ahead of them in some things, though in other things they were ahead of us. I made a sandwich of the bread and prosciutto while they were waiting because I was really hungry. I left the cantaloupe for later. Lettizia tried to convince me to combine them; she took a piece of cantaloupe and prosciutto from my place and put them into her mouth. Watching her made me feel sick and I thought it was odd that no one said anything about her behaving so strangely. Then I saw people at other tables doing the same. Soon the waiter came with a hundred other dishes, and I was overjoyed to be going home the next day.

◎ ◎ ◎

I opened my eyes, and the room was awash in sunlight. Through the old familiar broken venetian blinds on the slanted window the light poured in and it took me a few minutes to adjust. My brother was asleep on the other bed. I was home, finally, my mother and Željka's sat on the third bed. They had coffee together every morning, one morning at our place, the next at theirs. This was always at about 7:30 on the days when we went to school, and on weekends or holidays it was while we were still asleep. They drank their first coffee in silence and if I woke I'd pretend to be sleeping. The only thing to be heard was "Hey," then the water boiling on the hot plate, each of them smoking two cigarettes, I knew this because I counted the clicks of the lighter flint, then a few sighs, maybe once, softly: "Fuck you, life," and "Bye." I used to wonder what kind of friends would sit there silently like they were tired of each other, but then again, they were always together and didn't mix much with anybody else or visit the other rooms. With eyes closed I waited for us to be alone to nestle my head into Mama's lap so she and I could snuggle before we went down to breakfast. The night before it was late when we got in and I hadn't even unpacked anything or shown them what I'd brought for them. When she saw the gaudy top with parrots, Mama laughed. "This is for me?" She was amazed. "Well it's what Marissa sent you, she wears one just like it," I said. "How could she wear things like this when she's so rich?" Mama couldn't stop laughing at the parrot while holding the shirt up in front of her and looking in the mirror. "Well it's super fashionable," I said. Her laughter swept up my brother and me and we didn't want it to stop so in the end we convinced her to try on the shirt and prance around the room like on a catwalk. She played it up and I screamed with laughter and joy. And my brother got a few cool things that no one here, or even in Zabok where he went to school, was wearing. He was pleased, he suddenly seemed to care about what he looked like. "And now enough's enough, we'll be late for breakfast," said Mama, her voice different.

⊙ ⊙ ⊙

While we were still in the bus on the way back to the hotel, Jelena and I'd agreed that the next morning we'd meet at breakfast and sit together. I came down to the restaurant with Mama and my brother and right away I saw her standing, tray in hand, at the head of the line. She'd put on her new high tops, the same ones I had. Burgundy Converse All-Stars. Mine were in our room and I was sorry. "There's Jelena," I said to Mama, hoping she'd say, "Why don't you go sit with her," but she just nodded. I cared about Jelena and me sitting together, even though I hadn't seen my family for two weeks. Jelena spotted me, we exchanged glances and were the only people in the world who understood each other. It was only us from the Political School who'd gone on the Italy trip. Her Italian family had been rich, too, and they'd bought her whatever she asked for. They also invited her to come back to them over the summer, to somewhere in Switzerland. Her real family was her mother and brother who both had diabetes. The three of them had barely escaped from the hospital on the day Vukovar fell, and her father was stranded somewhere, like mine, and listed as missing. Her brother was a few years older and he gave her a hard time, just like mine did me, so we had lots in common. Hers was a shade crazier and ate live fish on a wager, and when he went to the bathroom he'd always strip down buck naked, regardless of what he was doing, she saw him through the keyhole, and once he heated up a coin on the hot plate and pressed it on her hand. Mine bugged me but he didn't give me scars. I waited for some old lady ahead of me in line to move so I could get closer to the wall where the menus for the week were displayed. Hamburger and tea. That's what it said for today. The first time this had appeared on the menu, we'd all been thrilled that we'd be served a hamburger for breakfast the next day. Most of the kids were already at the restaurant by seven that morning and then they pulled a fast one on us for the first and last time. On each plate we were greeted by two thick slices of bacon—all fat, no meat. Brand name: Hamburger. The greasy cook said, "What's wrong? Ain'tcha ever heard of it? Grilled hamburgers? Now that's a laugh, ha ha ha!" Ever since that day we'd known anything was possible, and even if it was on the menu, they might not serve it, and the ingredients might vary. For example, if there was fish for lunch on Friday, we'd have pasta with cheese for dinner, though finding the cheese on the plate was a challenge; the nutritional substitute was tiny fish bones. The line inched slowly along, and across the partition I saw Jelena. At other tables were friends of ours, but she sat alone. We got to the end, to the bread and silverware, and I turned to Mama and said, "I'm going to sit with her." "But why? Didn't you and she have enough time to talk while you were . . . ?" She didn't finish. Off I raced, leaving her and my brother behind. I felt them watching me, surprised, because whenever it wasn't a school day we ate together. I sat across from Jelena. She said, "Ciao." I said, "Come stai?" "Bene, e tu?" Jelena shot back. Everybody was looking at us.

We were different.

◎ ◎ ◎

Summers in Zagorje inched by slowly. There were no rivers, no seashore, just lots of flies and the stink of manure, and that was the hardest to get used to. At least at night one could sleep well—said those who slept well. My mother couldn't, nor could Željka's. She'd toss and turn while my brother listened tensely to her sighs. Sometimes she smoked and I breathed a sigh of relief because I'd heard somewhere that smoking soothed the nerves, it wasn't super healthy but at least she'd feel calmer after. She'd go back to bed and calm down. She'd lie there, her mind elsewhere. My brother always slept with his back to us and his head under the pillow. Mama had been given sleeping pills by the doctor and she hadn't stopped taking them. I believe she scarcely slept. Every so often she'd talk about how she'd worked herself to the bone in Vukovar—at the factory, with us kids, with her mother-in-law—and her spirit would be deep asleep when the alarm clock went off at three thirty in the morning because they were still living with Granny and Grandpa then and the house was far from where she worked, and then you come home and it's cook for them all and do the laundry by hand. And now, here you are, so sleep. Sleep all day if you like, there's nothing here but the flies and the waiting. The waiting. We've waited. For Papa to come, for Vukovar to be freed, for us to move up on the waiting list for apartments. All those were things that nothing could be done about meanwhile, but wait. We tried. We made the rounds of the Red Cross, posted Papa's picture, asked others to look for the tanned man in an undershirt in the deep shade of the yard where the first *kulen* of the year was on the grill for my ninth birthday. Nowhere was a man found who looked like him. We paid for an ad in *Arena* magazine, for anyone to contact us, anybody with knowledge of a man with this first and last name. No one responded, and then one day Mama received a marriage proposal in the mail, probably inspired by the ad. We stopped posting it. We stopped going to exchanges because the exchanges came to an end. All the living had already been exchanged. The occasional person for whom all hope was lost turned up years later, working as a slave on a remote farm in Serbia, cut off from the world, unaware the war was over. He wasn't even among them. The last person to see him in a vision, Fatma Nur Džennet—and what she saw wasn't totally clear—said she saw him as if he were under water and in a fog—but still alive, she added, at Mama's prompting of course. The last person who told us something about him spoke to us over the phone while we were freezing in a phone booth in the Zagreb main square; Mama dictated seven, six, one, nine ... the man was Alen, a numerologist from Rijeka. None of us understood much about numbers, math was always our weak point, but with the current madness it was inevitable that we'd come to believe numbers held the secret of the universe. Or of my father. Nothing happened and nothing changed. Time passed. On a few occasions word circulated through the hotel that Vukovar had been freed. I happened to be partway through an episode of *Beverly Hills, 90210* and near the front desk one time when that happened. Men began to gather and out-shout each other. Jelena and I rolled our eyes because they'd spoiled one of our rare pleasures—enjoying the series together; we didn't feel like watching it up in the rooms because of our brothers and mothers. As the men grew agitated, we began to take an interest in what was happening, and then little Darijan flew out of the crowd and declared: "We're going to Vukovar tomorrow!" Jelena told him, "Poor little thing!" He was two years younger than us, and I said to him, "Take a walk, blockhead!" By then I talked like that. "No, but really, really!" he shouted. "Ask anyone you like." We came closer to the frenzy and managed to catch phrases like *Croatian Defense Forces*, *unit*, *break-through*, and *America*, and that was enough for us to race off to our rooms and our mothers. When I came in, I saw her sitting in the half-light by the window, crocheting. Since we'd moved here, a tower of white yarn had grown in the cupboard, crocheted into flowers, doves, olive branches, and Mama came up with her own designs. This was all the rage among the widows or soon-to-be widows, it was even more than the rage. It became the currency brought to all meetings with members of the commissions, housing and otherwise, that ran our lives; a misplaced stitch might tip the scales one way or the other. This was the one thing she couldn't be distracted from and it soothed her like a cigarette. "Mama," I said; she didn't answer. "Mama," I said, louder. "Somebody downstairs is saying the city has been freed and return is a sure thing now." "Stop it," was all she said. "I didn't make it up, everybody downstairs is talking, there has to be something to it," I pleaded. "If there were, the Slovenes would already have said something." She looked up from her crocheting and shook her head.

She was right, of course. Not only did we not go home the next day, it felt like we never would. The words *housing commission* had the ring of something to be uttered in a church or at a university. The president himself, who chaired the housing commission, loomed as vast as a mountain and as friendly as an uncle who's never been near, but we all know he's out there somewhere, and his warmth reached back into the past, before we started saying *putovnica* instead of *pasoš*, and now he warmed us like a legend. Our day would come and we, too, would be granted an apartment. Resolve the housing problem. Resolution. For other kids my age, a word having to do with New Year's; for me it meant documents. Our Disability Resolution, our Pension Payments Resolution, our Resolution for Croatian Defender Status. The person heading the commission changed from time to time, but, as far as my mother was concerned, every functionary who held it could have had each square inch in each room of their apartment or vacation home carpeted with crocheted rosettes, if they liked.

Mama volunteered at Apel, the human rights center housed in a rented office near the Črnomerec barracks where the staff were searching for our nearest and dearest. She hoped that by being there she'd be close to those deciding our fate, just in case. She collected documents about the missing and they'd take them to the various embassies. She also worked at Uncle Grgo's, so often she'd go off in the morning and come back late at night. Sometimes with a white sack of bulk chocolate-covered cherries, or a package of broken cookies. During school vacations she'd take me along. First we'd go to Apel. Auntie Zdenka, who was in charge there and whose brother went missing somewhere near Osijek, always offered us cookies and coffee. The coffee was brewed on a little stove in a saucepan and they'd top it up from time to time. Two other women were usually there. Rosana from Bosnia, who did her nails in red but almost always gnawed them to the quick, was something like the secretary. The other was a woman of about seventy who'd lost her whole family, and she'd kiss and hug me and invite me to sit beside her. Aside from them there were always people I hadn't seen before; all of them were searching for somebody or something. Out of the whole morning we'd spend there, I'd be fine, no sweat, for a half hour with them in the office, meeting the new people and hearing their story, why they were crying. Then I'd start fidgeting and shooting glances at the door to the next room, which was kept dark and was filled nearly to the ceiling with boxes stuffed with documentation about the missing, imprisoned, killed. This room was thrilling for me both for all the boxes and for the computer. After I'd been fidgeting for fifteen minutes or so, Auntie Zdenka would ask, "What's up, kid, bored?" I'd smile and just happen to glance over at the door again. "What about a little time on the computer?" "Well, sure," I'd answer happily. "Just don't wreck anything!" she'd call after me. "I won't, I won't," I'd answer from the dark.

At school I'd already had a computer class; solitaire was my favorite game. After the packs had been cut a few times on the screen, I'd turn to the cardboard boxes and start digging through them. I went by alphabetical order, searching for familiar names, relatives, or people from my building. Sometimes I looked only for women, or boys the same age as my brother. Kids were the fewest in number on the list, but there were some. The youngest was born in May 1991 and died in November 1991. The oldest man on the list was born in 1898 and killed at the same time as the youngest. My folks were early in the alphabet, B. A., born 1953, Svib, Imotski, last seen November 18, 1991, at Vukovar General Hospital, all trace lost. He had a brother, I., and married wife A., who bore him two sons, J. 1975 and I. 1982. B. M. born in 1927, Svib, Imotski, killed on Priljevo in October. This is literally what it said. That was all that was known about my father, and there I was, the second "son": I. 1982. They gave no details, yet details seemed necessary because not everybody had died the same way, for instance, my grandfather's throat was slit, the baby died of an infection like lots of other kids at the Vukovar hospital because there was no longer any electric power, water, or medicine. Some people were hit by shells, and surely some died of natural causes. "So, are we off?" Mama would poke her head in at some point. "We need to get to Kvaternik Square before three. Have you made a mess in here with the papers? Please don't, we wouldn't want to lose anything." Everything could be so easily misplaced. What possible chance could this mountain of loose sheets of paper in boxes have, when nobody knew where so many people were? Once Auntie Zdenka organized a meeting with all the ambassadors in Zagreb who agreed to attend, and I was there. There was talk about the association, the ways in which the embassies might help locate the missing and obtain information about them from the other side. In the middle of the room around a large oval table sat fifteen ambassadors and a few women from the association. I sat behind some of them on a chair against the wall and waited for my moment. I was fascinated by their nearly identical polished shoes. At the end of the meeting Auntie Zdenka said, "Since we're asking for your help, we'd like to give you something in return." I got up and approached the first ambassador, who was sitting in front of me. The man was caught by surprise and was about to stand and turn, but I put my hand on his shoulder and said, "Sit." I was quite confident in my role and before he understood what I was doing, a gold chain with a four-leaf-clover pendant was around his neck. I smiled at him and moved on to the next. I fastened one on each ambassador, and in the end they all clapped for me and went home happy with their new gold chains. They were all impressed with me, too.

To step out of the dark, crowded, yet empty, room at Apel onto Ilica, the bustling Zagreb thoroughfare, was remarkable. The city was lovely and totally insensitive. They didn't need us, there were enough people in Zagreb already; they felt that being from Zagreb was a matter of some prestige. We rarely took a seat on trams, especially at first, we never stopped in city parks to do whatever people do when they're at the park. We never went to the movies or a theater, explored unfamiliar streets or discovered lovely spots. That's not why we were here. We made the switch to *salty rolls* but when we said the words they sounded off, always with a twang; when we bought them the baker had a little sneer. Like it was something so enormous, not a stupid doughy roll. But say it right. The only places we knew were the small, smoky cafés at bus stations because the bus ran only four times a day and in winter we needed a place to wait. We resided at a few locations in the city: the Zagreb Vukovar office, the Apel center, Grgo's office, and the housing commission office on Čerina Street. The street's name, Vjekoslav Čerina, rolled off our tongues naturally, like we were speaking of an old friend, and no one ever wondered who this man actually was. The name sounded like a savage's, and not, perhaps, a mild-mannered savage, but one who had taken scalps in war. Čerina.

A phone call for us. They called the front desk and left a message from the housing commission. Have the lady call this office so we can resolve her problem as soon as possible. We didn't sleep that night. Even in this country, we felt, things were finally moving in the right direction. We'd battle our way forward and it still wouldn't be easy but somebody was thinking of us and we'd be proud we'd sacrificed ourselves for a society where you don't need friends in high places to get things done. That's how we talked long after we'd put out the light. I was feeling a little sad about leaving because Jelena, Marina, Vesna, Ivana, and I were inseparable, and coexistence with the Piglets was finally bearable. The only thing I didn't regret was that Damir had found himself a Miss Piggie, one of the richest in the school, though she wasn't even pretty. I'd thought he and I might hook up. During every recess we'd watch each other and whenever he was near me he'd talk really loud and turn to see if I was watching. I did the same and kept vying for his attention.

I felt I was his true and secret love though he was the one who switched girlfriends all the time at school; he was the cutest boy. Still, I was convinced that I needed burgundy Levi's for success. But I couldn't face asking Mama to buy them for me, knowing my brother had come unhinged a few weeks before. I hadn't noticed, but I'd heard Mama talking with Željka's mother. She told her he came home from school all broken up and miserable. "He was snapping at everything and scribbling things in his notebook. He's talking less with me, he chokes it down. I ask whether he's dealing with problems, a girlfriend, maybe, something like that, I know I'm not Papa, but I'll do what I can. And then he bursts into tears. He's shaking all over. He said he's had it with this dingy room, he can't stand me like this and he's ashamed because he doesn't have the pocket money for a cola with his friends." Then Mama began sobbing, saying she was doing all she could and she couldn't take it anymore, and Nana and Granddad were here too and they couldn't look after themselves, let alone give her a hand. And in the end, she cursed my father for not leaving Vukovar with us. That didn't sound fair to me. I waited for things to quiet down a little, and then as everything was humming along with Damir I went into action. One afternoon, when I was home after school, I said, "You know the Levi's Marina has, her 501s, all faded and just a little flared? Her aunt brought them to her from Germany." I was immediately sorry I'd mentioned Marina's aunt because I had an uncle in Germany, and if she thought of him, things would probably go downhill. "You want Levi's?" Her crochet hook stopped and she shot me a sidelong glance. "Ones like that cost a hundred Deutsch marks for sure." I looked over. My tone, heavy on the melancholy, generally produced the best results; I had nothing left to say but: "I like the burgundy ones best, but there probably aren't any like that here." The last thing I expected was Mama coming back from work the next evening holding a bag with "Levi's" written on it. She came into the room cheerier than usual, which was already a gift. "I have a little something for you," she said, grinning. I couldn't believe it, I thought I'd burst with joy. She pulled the jeans out of the bag and it really did say Levi's on them, but under the light in our room they were actually more cherry colored than burgundy. And when I held them up, they leaned toward carrot and were just a smidge too big. Fine, I'm still growing. Mama watched me, elated, and said, "Come on, try them on. I think they'll be just right, I found them marked down at Varteks." My brother's were blue, a little weird, but still—Levi's. "There, son, the saleslady told me the kids are snapping them up." She was quiet for a moment, and then added, "Grgo gave me a raise." "They're super!" I said and kissed Mama on the cheek, even though they weren't really. "They're snapping them up because they're cheap," said my brother and put them away in the cupboard. I couldn't wait for morning. I lay there wide awake, imagining Damir and me walking down the school corridor holding hands. I didn't miss a detail. Of course I was wearing my Levi's, my burgundy Converse All-Stars I brought from Italy and my new burgundy turtleneck. I really liked that color. Everything was perfect till the moment when we each had to go off to our classrooms. At that point things got a little complicated because I wanted to skip the piece with the French kissing, and I'd already seen Damir do that with each of his girlfriends. He was, after all, in the eighth grade while I was in the sixth, though some of the sixth-grade girls had already tried it. Since he obviously loved me, I felt it wouldn't be too much to ask for us to put that off for a couple of months till we got to know each other better. By then I'd already be nearly a seventh grader and it probably wouldn't make me quite so sick.

With these thoughts I fell asleep and in the morning everything went just as it had in my dream until I walked into school. We ran into each other straight away, and he winked at me and nodded. He was standing by the girls' bathroom, he seemed to be waiting. Just when I was about to slow down and say hi, out came Miss Piggy and he put his arm around her neck. As if somebody had kicked me in the gut. I didn't expect he'd do that; I was always hearing him tap on the wall between our rooms. It occurred to me now for the first time that the tapping might have been his little sister. I wanted to weep, but I lifted my head up high and on I went. Miss Piggie, horror of horrors. But she was a seventh grader and probably let everyone stick their tongue down her throat. The thought of that consoled me and I convinced myself that I was better. I decided I wouldn't do that till I was married. It's disgusting and besides you're never sure if somebody loves you for who you really are.

The next day was the day of the phone call. We'd get an apartment in the nick of time, I'd have my own room and forget Damir, I hoped. Mama went off by bus at 7:00 a.m. She didn't know when she'd be back, but she said we shouldn't start packing without her, because we might not be going right away. I sat on the stoop out in front of the hotel and waited for the bus at 3:00 and then the one at 6:00. She came at 8:30, and we were in the room, though not in bed, because we didn't want to receive news like that in our pajamas. She'd barely opened the door when we were all over her,

"What happened, what did they tell you? When are we going?"
"We're not going anywhere," answered Mama. My brother and
I looked at each other and stopped talking, and she, instead of
sitting down, dropped straight onto the bed. "There are no apartments available in Zagreb or the surrounding area. I told them
I'd agree to something smaller, but they say there is nothing."
"Well then why did they call you?" growled my brother. Mama
said nothing for a minute, then all in one breath she said, "They
offered us a place on the island of Vis, I refused, what's the point
of going there, there's no school, hardly a living soul, and how will
I hear anything about him. And what if he turns up? If they like
it so much why don't they live there. I pleaded with them and
prayed, all that matters is a roof over our heads, we have to stay
nearby, I marched off to the president's office, I waited for him all
day, they said he wasn't there and then I saw him, just let me speak
to him, hear me out, nothing more. 'What's the rush, ma'am?'
That's what he said to me. 'You'll be going back to Vukovar, we
aren't waging this war for nothing.'" She jumped up and went into
the bathroom. My brother grabbed his jacket and stomped out,
slamming the door. I was left alone. It's the hardest when they
turn you down the first time, afterward you get used to it, and you
don't care.

⊙ ⊙ ⊙

Zagreb, June 12, 1995

Dear Mr. President!!
    At the outset I must tell you that I was driven to write this letter
by great sorrow and sore disappointment. Believe me, I no longer

know whom to turn to, so, placing my faith in your goodness, I am setting out my predicament for you.

In regard to this I would request that you find the time to read this letter to its end, because this is not just about me, and please do not hold against me any clumsiness. This is the first letter on such a subject I have written, and for a special reason.

I am the son of a Croatian defender from Vukovar who is missing in action, and I am currently housed at the CROATIAN ARMY Center (the former Political School) in Kumrovec, with my mother and sister. I wish to write to you about my pain, I have confided it to no one and I'm asking you for help because I believe you can help me. The first thing that hurts my feelings so deeply is the war profiteering in our country. Many people who until a few years ago were—and I apologize for my language—lowlifes, are now amassing a vast fortune, to the detriment of most honest, hard-working people. But, so it is. There is a saying, "One man's curse is another man's blessing." However, what hits me hardest and hurts the worst, I daresay, and is crushing the lives of family members of the imprisoned and missing defenders is the impression of the almost total disinterest and the unprotective attitude of most of the Croatian government and public toward us, when we are, in my opinion, because of our legally unregulated status, the part of the population that has endured the greatest suffering. I take upon myself the right to speak in the name of the other children (though children in name only because we were forced to grow up at age fifteen, and some much younger) and ask you to help us live lives of dignity, since we were unable to experience the most wonderful years of childhood the way other children our age could. It has been difficult every evening to stay up late so we could watch Slikom na sliku (in hopes of hearing news about our fathers), and then get up early and go off to school. After school to come back to our little room, barely nine by nine feet, finding our mother with tears in her eyes, all the life drained from her because of our father, and eating the lukewarm or even cold serving of meat (if you can even call it a serving for its size) that we were given for lunch. It was even harder because we could see Mother suffering that she couldn't warm it up for us, but we have no stove. After lunch it was time for homework, then supper, and then back to Slikom na sliku, and so we have done day after day, year after year. There were months when we literally slept on the floor, during which time I probably contracted bronchitis. I think under circumstances such as these any child who completes their schooling without succumbing to one vice or another is a Croatian hero on a par with his father in the war zone. Most of us before the war knew nothing of poverty, but when we lost everything we understood the difference between what it means to have and what it means to have not. In those moments we were always thinking of our father and his return, while many others were focusing on the paperwork for importing merchandise, apartments, medals, and I don't even want to think about what else. We want you to know you can find your strongest support for the prosperity of the homeland right in the segment of the population I consider myself to be a part of—the families of Croatian defenders. All this time, we have been patient and waited with love, and this for us now is very, very trying. We feel marginalized from almost everything going on in society, we feel discarded and forgotten. I was thinking about what my father would say if he knew of this. What would he say if he heard that when I asked for help, they answered, "So why did they go to war anyway?!" And, indeed, I too could ask why! But, no, I'm ready, if need be, to go tomorrow, not because

I have no choice, but for the same reason my father did. He was able to choose, he was a sales clerk and would have had a job in Zagreb, but he said: now or never, just like the song, and chose to put our homeland first. I want to bring your attention to a sort of epidemic that has been hitting the families of missing defenders since the fall of Vukovar, and that is that they have regularly been taken off the Defense Department payrolls (not everyone, only the ones who have no friends in high places). That's how we spent eight months without a single dinar, except the displaced-person allowance, which is only 100 kunas per person, and before it was even less, but still this is my homeland and I love it, and if I am able to I wish to help it when I complete my studies. I aspire to shoulder the responsibility of building our country with others my age, but how can I when we are not on a level playing field.

I am asking you to help us, give us a chance to express ourselves because we will never attack our homeland or leave it in the lurch. I am not seeking praise, just respect and help. I am asking you to help us solve our big problem, and that is our housing problem, as soon as possible because I wish to earn a university degree, and under these conditions I cannot study (my grades at the gymnasium were excellent). I don't know how we can realize our right because Mrs. S. K. from the Defense Department housing commission said there are no criteria for granting apartments, but we submitted our petition years ago, in 1991.

In this little room in Kumrovec it's hard, we have a table, three beds, and three hearts beating and yearning for your help, and you are, it would seem, our last hope. If we were pushed out of Vukovar, don't let us be pushed out of Croatia, we should have our place under the Croatian sun. The worst for me would be to be forced to go abroad to earn a crust of bread for my mother and sister.

I want to thank you for having read this letter and please accept my apologies if I have taken your time. This is, I believe, the most sincere letter I have ever written.

Thank you in advance, sincerely yours,

J. B.

CROATIAN ARMY Center p.p.21

41295 Kumrovec

I knew my brother was super smart, but that he could come up with a letter like this on his own was more than I could have hoped for. I was certain, if the president read his letter, that we'd be given an apartment. I read it over and over till I'd memorized it all, I was so proud.

○ ○ ○

I saw Igor for the first time at the Oaza disco club. Not long before, Marina and I had been playing Barbies in her room every morning, and lighting candles every afternoon for the late great Kurt Cobain. On the day he killed himself, her sister, two years older than us, sobbed, hysterical and disconsolate, threw us out of the room; we had to admit we were still kids who couldn't understand such pain, but we were also totally thrilled; she'd given us a glimpse at a whole new world we now wanted to be part of. For hours we played and rewound the cassette and yet never once did we ask what "Come as you are" meant, what mattered was to memorize every word, even if we didn't get them right. We wrote them down the way we heard them and that was enough. It was our first step toward the world of grown-ups. We walked into Number Seven without a knock and I'd cooled off on Damir and then one afternoon around the Easter holidays he wanted to shove his tongue into my mouth when he stank of onions. And besides he adored Tony Cetinski and DJ Bob and wore clothes from WGW. At the New Year's party the year before I'd danced a slow dance with him to "Plamen ljubavi," and now we all despised it while we flicked our hair over our faces and hummed Azra's "A šta da radim." The clothes from Caritas were no longer humiliating, there were interesting pieces to salvage in various states of disrepair, exactly what we were looking for. Our mothers clutched their heads, and so did others when we walked by, and that's what we wanted. I rummaged through Nana's cupboard and was surprised at how much grunge was in there, I was most intrigued by a lilac-colored wool dress in a plaid pattern with a high waist. And when Mama told me I wouldn't be going with her to Uncle Grgo's in Zagreb to pick up my new shoes for the season dressed like that, I snapped back that I didn't want his shoes anyway, the only shoes I'd wear were Docs. I have no idea how I spoke to her like that, and I must have really jolted her because next she was the one to surprise me: on Monday I walked into class wearing new dark-blue steel-toed Docs. The teacher looked at me in amazement and I said I'd forgotten my change of clothes. I could be forgiven because I'd never done it, at least not deliberately. As soon as I sat down a note was passed to me from Antolić that said: "My old man has boots like that for mucking out the pigsty." I turned and saw him sneering. "Zagorje hick," I almost said aloud, thinking there surely could be no salvation for this corner of the world. What could this miserable creature know about anything if he'd never even heard of Nirvana. Dumb Piglet. What I'd begun longing for was much farther from the time and place where I happened to be, and the closest thing to it in this mangy little backwater was Igor. His only bad side was that he was born in Zagorje, but thank heavens, his father was from Slavonia; once we found that out there was no longer anything preventing a fatal romance. Before I'd seen him, I'd heard of him from Marina's older sister. He was difficult to bump into just anywhere, he was already going to a high school that specialized in ceramics, but on Saturdays he was always, without exception, at the local disco, the Oaza. It had turned into a kids' club, because nobody else would be caught dead there. But for teenagers it was the only place to have fun. I knew the hardest part was yet to come, and this was to convince my mother she should let me go there one Saturday, just one, and then I'd never have to go anywhere again for the rest of my life. That was, roughly speaking, my argument. I'd need more of one, and Marina's parents weren't indifferent as to where she went, either, though her sister had already made the leap into the Oaza. My brother was useless because he couldn't care less about going out with friends, smoking and drinking, and everything else a boy his age was supposed to do. So we came up with a plan. When I pleaded with my mother to allow this last thing in my life, I'd tell her Marina's dad was letting her go, and if he heard from Marina that my mother gave me permission, he'd come at midnight to pick us up, though the disco was right around the corner from the Political School. Meanwhile Marina was batting her eyelashes at her dad while she explained to him that my mother was letting me go only if Marina could, and if he came to pick us up at midnight. He agreed almost immediately and everything would have gone smoothly if at that very moment the phone hadn't rung. Of course my mother was on the line, she'd probably sniffed out our ploy by instinct though this was the first time I'd ever lied to her, and she wisely sensed it wouldn't be the last. They realized we were pulling a fast one but we were still adorable and with the mitigating circumstance that until that time we'd never misbehaved, to our amazement, they let us go.

⊚ ⊚ ⊚

It was a spring evening and, for once, the air wasn't rank with the pigsties across from the hotel, we could smell a pinkish cast to the sky, and we tasted a totally new flavor of excitement. Of course it was chilly and of course I'd left my jean jacket in Marina's room because the slim cotton sweater looked way too good, and the pants were worn through on the butt and besides where would I have left it while I was dancing. Over my shoulder I carried a blue leather clutch and I was feeling practically thirteen, sometimes it felt like that, exactly like that. When we raced down the stairs and found ourselves outside on the road, Marina removed something carefully from her pocket, giggling, and tucked it into my clutch. "Hey, what's up, what's that?" I asked. "Oh, it's for later and if someone should ask." She was holding two York cigarettes she'd pocketed from her sister. I, too, laughed because it'd never occurred to me to smoke, but tonight it all made sense. The Oaza opened at 10:00 p.m. We were in front at ten till because at midnight we'd have to go. We were almost the first ones there and pretended we were out for a stroll until enough people had gathered that we could go in. We didn't want to be lame. Through the murky colored glass we could see the outlines of heads at the bar so we decided: "Let's go," I said. For the first time in my life I smelled the sweetish reek of stale smoke and alcohol and it made me dizzy. From that evening on, excitement had the flavor of vodka juice and laughter through coughs over a crumpled York. It was the beginning of freedom and pain.

Two older men were sitting at the bar; one was a puny guy, patched together, maybe a little slow, you couldn't tell his age. As soon as they noticed us they began chuckling. "Hey, girlies, wanna dance?" wheezed the little rat, narrowing beady blood-shot eyes. "Come'ere, come'ere," the yellow teeth beckoned, we pretended not to hear. We were disappointed that aside from them, the two of us were almost the only people there, but being in this legendary place that put us on a par with grown-ups, even if it was only grown-ups like them, was a genuine thrill. We sat in one of the booths and ordered colas. The room filled slowly, and Marina figured this was the right moment for us to smoke. She'd already tried smoking before but didn't like it so she held the cigarette between two fingers and tapped at the ash. She offered me one but I didn't want it. One of my brother's buddies might see me and tell him, and then I'd be in trouble. I thought I saw one of his friends, there were kids his age around. On the podium were little guys in rubber boots who'd come straight from the barnyard, there were babes wearing blue eye shadow and batwing sleeves, Piglets and Piggies of all shapes and sizes, but no one good-looking or a slick dresser. Either there weren't any like that, or they'd be arriving later. Our Vukovar crowd was there, too, and I could spot them easily. The boys: collar up, sweatpants, perfectly white sneakers. The girls: tight Levi's, dark, close-fitting T-shirts. Not to our taste. We got up to go to the restroom so we could check out whether anybody new had arrived. By then the place was crowded and as we made our way to the bathroom door, I saw him. There he stood, leaning against a wall, alone and so good-looking it hurt. Different. Long curly hair flopping across his boyish face, not because he still looked like a kid, but he was pale skinned, with big blue eyes, a little snub nose. I knew he was definitely the closest we could come to Cobain in Zagorje. "See him? Holy shit," said Marina. "Hey, watch your language, sure I saw him. Cute," I shot back, still looking his way. He wasn't smoking or drinking, he stood there, leaning on the wall, his eyes half-closed, like he was pained by everything. You could see he'd figured it all out, he was misunderstood and unwilling to waste words. There was no one like him at the hotel or at school and we were ready. Marina had already perfected her hobo look, while I was still a mama's girl so I thought he'd notice her, but still I checked him out as we walked by on our way back to the booth. She, too, looked him over, all's fair in love and war. "Good evening, friends, and welcome to the Oaza disco club!" rang out over the speakers, we looked at the clock and it was a quarter to twelve. Time for these Cinderellas to go.

"Hey, up and at 'em, breakfast will only be served for another twenty minutes," said Mama. Her words sounded different than usual, like she was teasing me because I couldn't be stirred. I knew she was thinking about my night out and wanted it to be crystal clear that she wouldn't tolerate my sleeping in. Then and never again. But it wasn't just that I'd gone out. I'd been in bed just after midnight but couldn't fall asleep. I shut my eyes tight for ages, but my ears were still throbbing with the blaring music and the whole new world I'd tasted. Outside the hotel, over the fence, inside me. Little darling, baby sis, far away from Mama and my brother. I got up lazily and presented Mama with a bare-bones report. "Good, glad you had a nice time," she said in a careful voice and in her tone I could hear, unsaid, "Glad you had fun, but don't think you'll be doing this every Saturday." I knew my mother fairly well, as she knew me. "Your shirt's on inside out!" she called after me when I'd already closed the door. "Exactly."

Instead of going down to breakfast I went to Marina's room and knocked softly. No one answered so I cracked open the door and in the murk saw her and her sister each fast asleep. They had their own room, lucky girls. There was no one I knew eating at the restaurant, none of my crowd, only my brother, finishing his breakfast at a table with four chairs by the door to the terrace. At the hotel he had no crowd of his own, just Jelena's brother, who was a little weird. I think that's why others found him interesting, especially girls, though I couldn't see why. I was his opposite, and we steered clear of each other, especially in public. When we were in our room we fought. I sat alone at the other end of the restaurant and he nodded, registering me as he left. More and more he'd been saying I was stupid, and I'd been cultivating an air of indifference; I often shot back with retorts. The worst I'd come up with was that he was Satan, but only because he'd started saying mean things to Mama: that she was incompetent and that any eighth-grade idiot would have found an apartment and a job already. One evening he even slept on the armchairs by the front desk and didn't care when Mama pleaded with him to come back. That's when I said it. When I was little and he pulled my hair or teased me in other ways, I'd lie in bed, seething, and imagine him at sixty, limping with a cane, tripping and falling, and me, some ten years younger, standing to the side and smirking, never offering a helping hand. Then I'd remind him of all he'd done to me, turn, and go. Now I longed for him to graduate from high school and go on to the university, to a dorm, anywhere, and free us from his outbursts. He only ever seemed to pick fights, never lending a hand except for his letters, the only good thing he did. Not long after he sent the first one he received an answer in which they addressed him as sir and the head of the Military Cabinet issued its recommendation to the Defense Ministry that our family be helped and granted an apartment. Nothing came of it. We waited because we thought it might mean something. After the first, my brother wrote a second letter, and when I read it, I thought nobody would ever write back to us again.

August 24, 1995
Ministry of Defense
Welfare Administration
Deliver to: Head, Lieutenant K. Č.

Dear Sir,

   Enclosed please find a copy of the letter I received in response to a letter I sent to our president, Mr. FRANJO TUDJMAN.

   I have only one question: can you as head of the WELFARE ADMINISTRATION help and do you want to help my family and me solve our basic existential question? This is about an apartment. My father was taken prisoner on November 20, 1991, at the Vukovar hospital by Major Veselin Šljivančanin and the Yugoslav People's Army. Nothing is known about what happened to him or many others, he was a member of the Croatian Army and he never left Vukovar; he stayed there as did many others to the very last. I know we are not the only case, but I also know that many other petitions were resolved long ago.

Why didn't you feel the need, after my letter addressed to our president, to call me or my mother, consider our problems sincerely, and try to do something to help us deal with the problem?

Mr. Head, you spoke with me and my mother when you were at the Apel center. My mother came to see you at your office after you became head of the Welfare Administration. Our names are in your diary, you promised you'd look into the files and make an effort to resolve, at last, the cases from 1991.

The president's office referred us back to you. And you and we received the letter the copy of which I am enclosing, and I am asking you: What now?

My father is not by my side to help us, your children have you, you love them and care for them, but please remember my sister, mother, and me and the other families who have suffered as we have.

Sincerely,

J. B.

CROATIAN ARMY p.p. 21

41295 K.

However only a few days after my brother sent the letter, he received an answer. It said:

August 30, 1995
Ministry of Defense Mr. J. B.
Welfare Administration CROATIAN ARMY *Home p.p. 21*
Zagreb 41295 K.

Dear Mr. B.

On July 7, 1995, we received your letter addressed to the president of the Republic of Croatia, Dr. Franjo Tudjman, with the petition to help you regulate your regular payments and your housing problem.

The Act on Amendments to the Rights of Croatian Defenders from the Homeland War entered into force on the day it was published in the Official Gazette, on June 1, 1995.

Because, pursuant to this act, the families of Croatian defenders imprisoned or missing are treated as having rights equal to those of families of Croatian defenders killed, we find it necessary to inform you that you have the right to:

payment in the sum of family pension,

payment in the sum of family disability.

The procedure for exercising this right must be begun at the Directorate for Defense welfare office nearest to your place of residence. Please enclose the following documents with your petition:

a certificate of the Commission for Imprisoned or Missing Persons from the Government of the Republic of Croatia that unambiguously certifies the identity of the person who is imprisoned or considered missing;

a certificate of membership in a Croatian Army unit as well as status (rank, duty) — to be obtained from the Defense Directorate;

a certificate confirming the pension base (the basic wage for December 1994) — for cases to date, and the same will be officially requested from the Defense Directorate Personnel Administration, Zagreb, Stančićeva 6;

birth certificate (marriage certificate);

certificate of nationality;

registration of place of residence (residency);

certificate of circumstances of disappearance or imprisonment (request these from military unit).

As the Welfare Department does not have the authority to

resolve housing issues, please return to the Housing Administration of the Ministry for Defense and solve the problem therein.
  Sincerely yours,
  HEAD OF THE WELFARE
  DEPARTMENT FOR THE WOUNDED
  Captain A. K. M.

And then, again, nothing.

◎　◎　◎

I was sorry Marina and I weren't speaking. The last thing she said, through Jelena during recess, was that I got on her nerves because nobody ever saw me as a loser even when I was carrying around the Barbie bag I used last year, while she was teased mercilessly by everybody, and anyway she was the first who'd heard about Igor. But though I was sorry about her, I was thrilled when Igor sent me a message through his sister to say I was sweet and we should go out for coffee if we ran into each other again at the Oaza. Now I was faced with a dilemma. How could I keep Marina from being angry now that she, too, liked Igor, without me losing him? And if she wouldn't speak to me, how would I be able to reach out to her sister, who knew his friends and could hook us up? I walked home from school alone, I didn't need anybody because I didn't want to share my feelings. How cool it was to be all melancholy and sighs. The vestibule of the Political School was bathed in glimmering sun and all the glass and wood seemed warm. The only thing was all the dust visible in the air; after all these years the cleaning ladies were no longer vigilant.

Out of the enchanted dust swam a wizened, mournful face, frail little hands clung to my neck. Marina's grandmother wailed and I was totally taken aback and it was incredible, all of it, especially because of Marina and Igor. After a few minutes I began to catch some of what she was saying and realized this had nothing to do with Igor. "Condolences, condolences," the old woman chanted, kissing me and clinging. Granddad had been in the hospital for a while, a mental hospital. I was hoping it was he who'd died, not someone else. "Your granddad's gone" confirmed my suspicions. I felt a wave of relief, but her sobs and how crazy in love she was with Granddad, and the thought that he'd never again send me to the bar to bring him a beer—even though I'd been resenting that recently and sometimes asked another kid to go—sent me into sobs, bitter sobs. Toward the end he'd started boozing even more. Whenever she came back from Zagreb, Mama was afraid of what she'd find. When he boozed he didn't do anything weird, mostly he just wept and then he'd want to kill himself. Always by electrocution, probably because he'd been an electrician and knew how to do it that way. Then Mama and Nana would plead with him, they'd drag him away from the wall socket and tuck him into bed. My brother went ballistic a few times and I thought he might punch Granddad, and the whole thing was a little embarrassing. Then he started muddling days and years so they took him to Jankomir. The doctor there suggested Mama was the crazy one, she was so eager to be rid of him. Then Granddad came back to the Political School and wanted to die but they didn't let him so on he boozed, and back he went to the hospital and now he'd died, just like that. From a pulmonary embolism, they said. In a few bounds I reached the first floor where Granddad and Nana lived, and all the way to their room I smelled cheese pastries and fritters. All the hot plates and toaster ovens on the floor joined forces when somebody died, the fuses would blow because everybody wanted to bring something. There were chairs in the dark hallway in front of their room and Nana, surrounded by women in black, was sitting on one of them. "Child!" burst out of her in the dark when she saw me. We hugged a long time and the others patted us and smoothed our hair. Everybody loved Nana, Nana didn't love Granddad, Granddad loved the ladies and the booze. He was good to me when I was small, but now, I didn't know. Nana cried, how could she cope alone, why hadn't he waited till they could go back to Vukovar together, but she was ready, they'd be together again one day in the home nobody could destroy. When Nana babysat for me when I was little, she never missed the funeral of a close friend or even distant acquaintance; she'd bring me along. I was intrigued to watch grown-ups cry and how they were suddenly so kind to each other. When the ceremony ended, Nana would always turn to face the newer part of the cemetery and say: "There, that's where our house is." I'd stand on tiptoe to see a roof, but I never saw anything. Only much later did I realize she was referring to their future grave. Now, having lost his home, Granddad wouldn't be put to rest in the house she'd imagined, but in the yellow dirt of Zagorje on a little hill by the church. Mama came back, dog-tired, on the last bus after the autopsy and the coroner, traipsing from one side of town to the other arm in arm with Željka's mother, the buses only intermittent. Into the room Mama stepped, haggard, at around ten, a bye was heard in the hall, the neighboring door clicked and then ours. My brother and I said nothing, we didn't know what to say, my condolences sounded forced, but, then again, he was her dad. "Are you okay?" I asked. "You're not sleeping yet," she answered. Lots of people were at the cemetery on the day of the funeral, nearly half my class came. The sorrow wasn't crushing so the special attention felt nice. Everybody was kissing us, squeezing our hands, eyeing us. Nana handled herself well, she cried a lot but softly, and she'd look each person who came over to her in the eye. She was a gentle woman and she loved people, needed them. Mama was dark, as dark as she could be. Enveloped in a deep blue funk, she didn't see anyone. When the funeral was at its peak, Nana's wails began raining down on us. "You were so good to me, you never made it back to Vukovar, why did you leave me, where will I go now . . ." and so on, round and round. Even I cried a little, but I was mostly watching Mama, who looked like she might crumble, she was watching Nana like Nana was about to pull free of her and fly off. When everything was over and the funeral-goers were dispersing, Željka's mother threw an arm around Mama's shoulders while she brushed her eyes with a sleeve, and all I heard Mama say was, "Did she have to keep saying how she spent her whole life with him . . ."

◎ ◎ ◎

That night after the funeral I slept in Nana's room so she wouldn't be alone. Her neighbor, Milka, stayed till late, I was drifting off to sleep and they still hadn't agreed on how long one isn't supposed to watch TV or listen to the radio, and how long to wear black. The customs varied from village to village. I didn't dare ask how much this carried over to the third generation. I lay on Nana's bed and thought about Granddad's plaid shirt that had been too small for him anyway—it reminded me of one I'd seen on Cobain—and Nana's ocher-colored sweater which would look great with it. Milka was all for two years in widows' weeds, and that suited me because of the yellow sweater, while Nana said the custom was a year, to which Milka retorted, "Sure, six months'll do if you've a mind to marry again." Nana lowered her eyes demurely and Milka said softly, "I'll be off now." Everybody knew Milka had been fooling around with Old Man Franjo. They didn't wait long after his wife Mara died. For a time such things circled through my mind. Limun and Ozrenka were railing at each other in the hall, she was pregnant, alone, no teeth and no schooling, all she had was Limun and he'd left her for a Zagorje girl. I wanted to go to the Oaza on Saturday for a Zagorje guy; on Granddad's bed Nana was sighing audibly, Granddad was six feet under, and despite it all, or maybe because of it, I felt so alive: I needed to come up with a plan.

After school I cruised around the halls of the Political School; I considered going down to the front desk to wait for Marina, she and Jelena weren't in my class and their school day went on longer. Aside from Nataša, the only one from the Political School in my class had been Ivan, but he stopped going to school and didn't do anything but steal, pick fights, and smoke. He wasn't as dense as little Mika, who idolized him. You could talk Mika into just about anything, even stealing from the rooms right next to his, though he could've had whatever he wanted because his dad had broken out of Vukovar and was working in Germany. Things disappeared from the rooms of the women with whom his mother drank coffee and everybody knew it was Mika's doing and Ivan had put him up to it. A few years later—when his family were among the first to return to their rebuilt house—the press reported that forty-three-year-old S. M. had robbed currency-exchange offices around Vukovar at gunpoint. Mika and his dad, this same S. M., had, so you see, been thieves since Mika was in diapers. There was talk for ages in the hallways, and women said Mika's mother had always been trash. You could tell. Everybody knew what she was up to while her husband was in Germany, she was a slut and the kid was a crook. Somehow it got out that Mika's little sister's pubic hair started growing while she was still in third grade. They were all creepy, but while they were living there they strutted around like they were better than the rest of us. "Hey, where are you off to?" I heard behind me after I'd walked by Ivan's room. "The front desk," I said and was about to continue walking. "Come in, my mom's in Zagreb." "I'm going down to wait for Marina," I said, hesitating. "Come here, see what I got." I didn't want to spar with him from the hallway and I was intrigued to see what he had to show me. "We were in down the village the other day, me and Miro," he began. Miro was like him, a little older, sallow and freckled, a bar hound by high school. I figured they'd swiped something again from the Marshal Tito living-history ethno village, probably something big, after everything small had already been stolen. This was nothing new. We girls wrote all kinds of things railing against the Serbs and Commies in the guest book, and once a TV show mentioned the comments as an example of the vandalizing of the Croatian cultural heritage. I wrote: *Comrade Tito, thanks a million, big of you to give the cute little room to my mother, brother, and me, rot in hell.* They quoted some examples on the show but didn't read mine. The boys first pilfered little stuff, but later they stole whatever they could drag out of there: plaster casts, a pig with an apple in its mouth from the wedding table in the little house exhibiting Zagorje wedding customs, rusty pincers from the make-believe Zagorje smithy, wooden toys Zagorje children were supposed to have played with, and other dumb stuff. The only place they couldn't get into was Tito's birthplace; guards were posted there. They were probably worrying we might make off with the big sculpture out in front. "So what did you do?" I asked. "We went out at night," grinned Ivan, "you know the sculpture outside? We dressed it up in Tićo's granny's nightgown." We both burst out laughing; that was so cool. "The guy who was on guard," he went on, "realized something was up and came out to see, threw a fit and started screaming at us, and meanwhile I snuck into his sentry booth." Ivan bent down and pulled something wrapped in a dishtowel out from under the bed. When he unwrapped it, I only realized after a minute that I was looking at a pistol, the genuine article. "You're nuts," I told him. "Hey, what if somebody tries to mess with me now?" "Put that away, you've gone too far." We looked at each other. "Gotta go, Marina's waiting." "You ain't goin' nowhere," he said. He started laughing and came over. My heart was in my throat. "One day you'll be my wife," he said. He shoved me hard with his shoulder and unlocked the door. I flew out and shouted, "Moron!" He just laughed, and I fled to my room.

◎ ◎ ◎

Slaven and Antonia were the grandkids of a Vukovar man. Everybody called them Zagi, or Zagorac, because their grandfather had moved to Vukovar after the Second World War, but he'd actually been born in one of the villages nearby. He, too, had suffered, but some of his childhood memories began coming back, he was always upbeat, looked like he'd gained a little weight, and his local twang resurfaced. His daughter, son-in-law, and grandkids had been housed at the Hotel Laguna in Zagreb, and sometimes they'd come out to visit. Antonia was my age and fit right in when we saw her that afternoon sitting on the steps to the restaurant. She was wearing white All-Stars and tattered shorts. I'd seen a tall boy as I left Ivan's room, he was going into Number Seven and lighting up a cigarette, and now it occurred to me that he might be Antonia's older brother. Marina saw him and forgot about being angry with me over Igor. He was wearing a leather Ramones jacket, his face all cheekbones and his fingers bandaged from playing the guitar. The misunderstood gaze, of course. He was really cute but I had no interest in getting to know him, et cetera, because I didn't want Marina to be angry with me again. It was Friday afternoon when they came, we heard he didn't have a girlfriend and he'd be here till Sunday night. Of course their granny would let the Zagis go to the Oaza the next day so we, of course, had to be there, too, and of course my mother would never in her wildest dreams imagine I'd ask for such a thing so soon after the funeral and everything. On my way to the room I was working up strategies for how to approach Mama about Saturday. Dumbelina appeared in the hallway near the service stairs, wiping her mouth as she left the restaurant, and hurried past me. "Hey, were you at lunch? What're they serving?" I barely had time to ask. She stared at me blankly, startled, and a tic she had with her lips started. It always did it when she was edgy, for example in class when the teacher called her up to the board, though nobody expected much from her. She'd open and close her mouth like she was yawning or her lips were bothering her. "Pasta with cheese, gotta go," she said and vanished around the corner. Now Tićo came from there, too, patting the stiff hedgehog-looking hairdo his mother gave his ash-blond hair. Tićo was the male version of Dumbelina, just smarter. He, too, was slow but he had a temper. His dad had died in Vukovar, he and his mother were alone, and she treated him like he was a grown man even though he was only a sophomore at the vocational school for carpentry. He was over six feet tall and always hanging around the basketball hoop out in front of the hotel, he didn't drink or smoke. His mother was crazy proud of him and was always going on about how her Tićo was so handsome and smart. It occurred to me that he and Dumbelina were up to something, but it seemed so incredible that she'd ever hook up with anyone, especially someone like him, that the very thought of it made me sick.

Igor. His long hair and his pale face. His hands, I had no idea what his hands were like but I liked thinking about them. He was cooler than everybody else around here. The room was locked and when I went in I closed the door behind me. I lay on the bed and shut my eyes. It was like someone else's hand slipped into my underpants, I didn't want to think about what I was doing, I just pulled the blanket up over me and gave in. When I came out from under the covers, my brother was sitting at the desk facing the wall. "A telegram came from Uncle, condolences for Granddad," he said coldly. I said nothing, I just smoothed the bedding and walked out. When I came back that evening a copy of *Super Teen* magazine was under my pillow. It was open to the "Questions and Answers" page. The article circled in red marker began: "I am fifteen and I don't have a boyfriend, but I masturbate every day and I can't stop, though I'd like to. Am I okay? How can I help myself? Miserable." I didn't read the answer. I wanted to die.

◎ ◎ ◎

It was Saturday around noon and I had no more time to delay. Mama was cleaning our room with the so-called hand-held vacuum. The device didn't have a proper name. It required no electricity; every well-equipped room in the hotel had one. It was hardly better than an ordinary broom and worse than a proper vacuum. And proper vacuums weren't used even by the people who could afford them; if two or three were plugged in along with a few electric kettles, the fuses would start blowing on our floor. The cleaning device had a box the size of a videocassette which was closed at the top; below there was an opening for a brush that spun around, scooping the larger crumbs into the box, though of course not the dust, but for our little room it sufficed. We had a red one, Nana's was blue. You could talk with the person while they were cleaning. It made no noise, only dust. "What's up, are you here to ask for something?" Mama looked up at me from where she was kneeling, picking up the hairs that the hand-held vacuum wasn't catching. She knew. She always knew, but I wanted to know, too. I tidied my things that all fit on one shelf and rummaged through my CDs. I had a dozen cassettes, but my three CDs were my pride and joy. On one, which I'd kept from the ZaprešiĐ library, there were covers of Beatles songs, while the second, the Doors, was given to me by a weird girl who was a friend of my brother's, I thought they might be dating but he was too shy to say so. The third I got from Australia, it was called

Happy Birthday, Ivana, and it was sent to me by some of Granny's old friends, émigrés who had a pop tamburitza ensemble. "I thought I might go out this evening," I said softly. "Didn't you go out last Saturday and say you'd never ask for anything ever again? And besides, we buried Granddad less than a week ago," she said, which was exactly what I'd expected. First she looked at me sort of implacably, but tired, and this was my space to maneuver. I kept still and waited. Nothing happened and she too was quiet. I fidgeted around the room, watched her out of the corner of my eye, sighed. When I was a kid, I used that look to get whatever I wanted out of Papa. Roller skates, ice cream, a trip to the pool. "You're my little scoundrel," that's what he'd say, and take me into his lap. With Mama I had less of a chance, she was the one in charge. Now, too, but more tired. "He'd have let me go," I whispered. "In your dreams. He'd have locked you up and thrown away the key, go ahead, see if I care!" she snapped. Not another word was needed, this was it, and I flew to Nana's room for the ocher sweater. When I came back, she looked like she'd been crying but I didn't ask. The bathroom where I was getting ready was so cramped that two people could barely stand in there together, but that was the last thing we'd've complained about. We knew there were twenty to a bathroom at the barracks, and the barracks were the bottom of the barrel in the life of displaced persons. At the other end of the spectrum was the Intercontinental Hotel in Zagreb. We were somewhere in between. Across from the bathroom there was a mirror in the hall so I took up nearly half the room with my preparations and couldn't avoid the barbs from Mama and my brother. My blue Docs, the ocher sweater, my T-shirt on inside out and my carefully uncombed hair struck a different note from my last time out, but I was working on a fantastic image. "You have nicer stuff than that," said Mama. "The perfect displaced person," interjected my brother caustically. "Well, that's what I am, moron," I retorted, so he recited in a moronic voice, "I'm a little refugee, a big, bad Chetnik man blew up my house." "Ha, ha," was all I said, why argue with him, we did that every day, endlessly, no matter how much we avoided each other, the farthest we could get from each other in this room was on our beds with Mama in between. He didn't have a clue about music, fashion, his girl-friend helped him some, but not much. Tonight he seemed to be in fine spirits, from Mama I heard that Uncle was in Zagreb and might come to see us the next day. That would've been a huge thrill if it weren't for what lay ahead that night; I'd think about Uncle tomorrow.

I left the room all dressed but only partway ready because we did our makeup in Marina's room away from their questioning eyes; she turned down the light in case one of her folks came by. It's not that we had much makeup to do, or that we even knew how to apply it, but we had Marina's older sister. A black eyebrow pencil and an almost used-up dark-red lipstick were what she'd left us, and we did the best we could. When we finally went downstairs at about nine to show off there was hardly any-body about. Only the occasional little old lady who hadn't yet retreated to her room and a kid here and there, the untended rug rats who were born here and knew only about scampering around the hotel halls, shinnying up the railings, and crawling in and out of all the Political School nooks and crannies. They were like no-see-ums, yet they served as the higher consciousness of our living space, well-adapted little cockroaches who knew their way around every conference room when they were still in diapers: baptized in one, at day care in the second, smoking their first cigarette in the third. They wrote to Santa that most of all they longed to go home. When the little Mihaljević girl said something to her dad with a Zagorje twang, he beat her something awful and she couldn't understand why. She was six and her sisters were five and two; after that they knew they must never use Zagorje dialect. Their dad was desperate for a son so every other year the family added yet another room. The middle girl, Dragana, was climbing around on the armchairs that evening and when she saw us she froze. Behind our backs we heard her voice, still in a baby's lisp: "You aw scawy." Rug rats. We left her, and through the fragrant evening air someone, drunk and young, ahead of us sang out the refrain: "Bolje biti pijan nego star."

In the dark of the disco club I couldn't tell whether Igor was there or not and my eyes were already starting to smart from the smoke and the squinting so I headed out for air. Suddenly I felt a light touch on my back, and when I turned, I saw him. He smiled and said hi. And I said hi. "On your way out?" he asked, looking me straight in the eye. "Yeah, the smoke's getting to me." Outside, we moved a few feet to the side and perched on a low wall. "I saw you here last Saturday," smiled Igor, he was really seeing me, I couldn't believe it, and meanwhile I was thinking about what to say. "Yeah, I was here, it's super, only the music's a little lame." From inside you could hear Coco Jumbo. "Right, my sister's boyfriend is the DJ, he has to spin this shit, but at around four he switches to Azra and Psihomodo Pop." I could only dream of the day I'd be allowed to be out until 4:00 a.m., but this would do for now, seeing him up close, having him smile just at me. "Can I bring you something? A beer? Vodka juice?" he asked, and behind him I thought I heard a voice I knew well. My brother. How I hated him; I'd been sure he'd come down to see what I was up to and embarrass me. He was headed our way and I knew he'd say something. Something stupid. "Mama's waiting for you, hurry home. Oh ho, look at that boy's hair! And I was thinking you were out with one of your girlfriends! Nobody can tell who's a boy or a girl anymore, ha ha!" he quipped and walked on by. I felt awkward and when Igor came back with the drink I downed it in a gulp for the first time ever, and when I noticed he was watching me in surprise and laughing, I said, "That's how I like it." "Tough cookie, eh?" he said. "Gotta go," I whispered, and when he offered to see me home I thought I'd swoon. The walk was short, we were swaying and he took my hand after a *Lepi cajti* country-music number. I stared straight ahead because it felt silly to be looking at him and smiling, and I was feeling woozy. We were standing out in front of the Political School when he moved in close, and I still hadn't figured out what was up when I felt his tongue in my mouth. Warm and moist, both the most thrilling and most disgusting thing I'd ever known. I was stumped, where to put mine? No one had told me about that part and I hadn't thought we'd be going that far. When he stepped back I was still frozen, and he asked, "Can I call you?" "Yes," I gave him the number, "and when the front desk picks up, ask for extension 385." "Extension? What's that?" he asked, surprised. "My room," I answered, "it's where I live."

⊙ ⊙ ⊙

Waking up this time was even more painful than it had been the first time. Željka's mother had already left and mine was pacing nervously around the room. I observed through half-open eyes that she was scraping our little white hot plate, she was being strangely loud about it, there was nothing left to scrape, and then I remembered Uncle was maybe coming today. It must be early still, nobody was sending me down to breakfast so I pretended to sleep a little longer. After tidying up, Mama sat across from me, sighing, and glanced at her wristwatch. Since we left Vukovar she'd never taken it off, she slept with it on, sometimes she'd sit there unbuckling and buckling the watchband. She'd been given the watch by Uncle's wife, the German lady, who didn't know how to say a single word in Croatian so that's probably why we called her Uncle's wife instead of Aunt, and besides she was only eight years older than my brother. Every summer when they visited, Papa'd be excited. He'd save the best prosciutto and *kulen*, and if Uncle, for instance, said, "That leather jacket is sharp," Papa would take it right off and hand it to his brother. Mama disapproved, but Papa protested, saying Uncle would do anything for him. Granny approved with a cackle, saying: "You have only one brother, but you can have as many wives as you like." Her attitude about Mama could be summed up in that one sentence. In the hotel restaurant where Papa worked, Uncle would be given the best seat, though Papa had to leave the tip afterward for the waiters. If Uncle's wife wanted to go to a disco, they all went to the disco. The summer before the war they were staying with us and while I was up in my room, dressing their poodle in baby clothes, I heard Uncle boasting about something that it could be dunked in water or smashed on a rock

but it would never stop working. I didn't hear Papa say anything, and then Uncle said, "There, little brother, it's yours." I
went into the room to see what Papa'd been given, and he was
gazing at the watch like I gazed at my huge stuffed Garfield.
Then Uncle's wife took off hers, a woman's version of the same
watch, and with a smile and nasal tone, she gave it to Mama,
who protested, "Nein, nein," and I thought, I have the nicest
family in the world. They were all so happy just then, all of
them but Gina the poodle who was yipping in the baby car-
riage. Now I'm not so sure.

At around 4:30, once the wait had drained away all our joy,
into the miniature bubble of our world strode Uncle through
the hotel room door. He was tall, tanned, nearly as handsome
as Papa. "Hello, hello!" he filled the room with his congenial
baritone. A man, not the one who'd gone missing, who'd disappeared, the one we were waiting and searching for, not quite,
almost, his blood, his brother. I jumped up to kiss him, he didn't
have to bend down, I'd grown, I looked him straight in the
eye. "Sit down, would you like something to drink?" Mama's
voice quavered with the excitement. "Sure, sure, coffee would
be great," drawled Uncle while Mama maneuvered around the
cramped space, from the hot plate to the cupboard, from the
package of coffee, to the box of cups, to the box of cookies.
"Nice, cozy, not a bit musty," said Uncle, pleased, like we'd been
living before in a basement. "I visited our aunt this morning,"
he said, meaning Granny's sister, "they're over in Špansko,
or whatever they call it, their room is bigger, but the bathroom, the bathroom is shared by like a hundred old codgers.
And it's pleasant around here, none of the, you know, traffic."
"How's your family?" Mama interrupted his assessment of our

accommodation. "Yeah, good, good. The kid was held back in kindergarten, they said he's maybe hyperactive, they're so strict there. And he's a little devil, I bought him these two turtles, you should see how they scuttle around his room. And the good lady, you know, she's always harping on about one thing or another, and, sure, she's getting fatter. She's fine, how else could she be." My brother laughed at first out loud, and then softer and softer. I didn't. Uncle had brought some bags with him and he began pulling out balls of socks, one after another, and handed them to my brother. I'd never seen so many socks. At the bottom were also two of his shirts. A little stretched, a little oversized. "You're broad in the shoulders," he grinned at my brother. "And here's something for our girl, you're so big now," he said and set on my lap a green package wrapped in transparent cellophane. In it, in an array of colors and shapes, were six little bars of soap. I'd been given little soaps. So now I was a big girl. What would a kid do with soaps? When the conversation lulled, he sighed and said, "What can you do, there's no shedding this skin of ours." Two or three seconds later I said, just loud enough so he could hear, "Some do." He turned to me and color flooded his smoothly shaven face. "They sent me packing, beat it or you're dead, I had to choose. They all knew me." I thought he'd go on but he stopped, halfway through a sentence, and I stopped, staring at the floor so I wouldn't have to look at them, at Mama and my brother. Soon we said our goodbyes and when he left, he took with him his voice, mood, jokes, ease, life.

◎ ◎ ◎

Ministry of Defense of the Republic of Croatia
Deliver to: Minister G. Š.

Dear Mr. Minister,

Please forgive me for taking your valuable time, I will be brief. Please help me solve what is such a huge problem for me, and that is my housing problem. I am from Vukovar, I have two children, and my husband, as a member of the Croatian Army, was taken prisoner at the Vukovar hospital and to this day, I'm sad to say, we know nothing of what befell him. We have been housed at the former Political School in Kumrovec in a tiny room for five years now. My son is twenty and studies in Zagreb, my daughter is thirteen and now she's finishing the eighth grade and should be enrolling in high school but there is no high school in Kumrovec. I submitted my petition for an apartment in 1991 and since then we have received nothing but empty promises that this problem would soon be resolved, so here we are still today in this little room in Kumrovec. Mr. Minister, sir, we went to you to ask for help once already and we approached our president as well and, believe me, we'd be most grateful if you and our president would send the housing commission a recommendation to grant us an apartment because they would obey you. We wrote to the president on June 12, 1995, and to you on November 23, 1995, as you will easily ascertain. After that we were sent a letter from the housing commission saying that as soon as the first housing unit became available they would resolve our case immediately, yet since then many people have been granted apartments. Mr. Minister, I came to see you once with a group of several wives and mothers from Vukovar and I remember your words well when, with tears in your eyes, you said: "Don't ask of me what I cannot do, but as far as your welfare is concerned, you are free to ask about that." I therefore resolved to ask you once again for help because I don't know what to do. It is terribly difficult for me to see my children so sad because I feel that though they lost their father they have the right to a life of dignity until they are able to look after themselves.

Thank you again!

A. B.

Ministry of Defense, Republic of Croatia p.p. 21 Kumrovec

◎ ◎ ◎

Housing Commission
To the President of the Commission
Mrs. I. P.

Dear Mrs. P.!

I know I am not the only woman who has not resolved her housing problem, but believe me I have been waiting patiently since 1991, and now I am truly suffering. I am housed in Kumrovec with two children in one small room. My son is studying in Zagreb, and my daughter has finished eighth grade and is about to enroll in high school. Since she finished all eight grades with straight As, she would like to enroll in a gymnasium in Zagreb because here in Kumrovec there are no high schools. I am the wife of a missing Croatian Army defender from Vukovar, and my father-in-law was killed in Vukovar, also as a member of the Croatian Army. Believe me it is much harder for the families of the missing because there are things we can never accept, and the uncertainty is crushing us. Mrs. P. I pray to you to help my chil-

dren lead lives of dignity because if their father were by their side
they would never be suffering as they are now.
    Thank you in advance!
    A. B.
    Ministry of Defense, Republic of Croatia p.p. 21 Kumrovec

◎ ◎ ◎

"Come on, are you done in the bathroom now or what?" my
brother banged at the door. A little longer, I'm in no rush, I said
to myself. I tucked the letters back into the blue envelopes and
wondered why Mama was writing them. My brother had always
been the one to do that before, but recently he'd gone off the
deep end so he'd probably caved. Maybe because he's a student
now at the university and thinks no one's his equal. Before, I was
the only stupid one, now Mama is, too, it's not enough that she's
always miserable, he has to knock her even further down. "Take
a computer course! Driver's ed! Folks with an eighth-grade edu-
cation are more capable than you! Go ahead, sit here and rot
in this room, why don't you, you've forgotten how to talk with
people," these were his most frequent barbs. She would edge
away and tell him to leave her alone. I could hardly wait for him
to move to a student dorm and stop with the complaining, but I,
too, would be moving soon to a dorm.

All my friends were boarding, everyone who wanted to go
on to high school or the university. My brother was in a university dorm, I would board at a high school dorm. I tucked the
envelopes into my pants so I could slip them back when no one
was looking, tuck them into our aunt's black briefcase where all
the documents and important papers were kept. Mama pho-

tocopied all our letters that had to do with the apartment or
Papa, fewer and fewer about Papa. So one day we'd have proof.
For whom and what, I couldn't say. As I walked out of the bathroom I jabbed my brother in the ribs with my elbow. "I can't
wait till you move out," I muttered and sat on my bed. Like so
many other times, I was saved by the Walkman I'd been given in
Italy and singer Djordje Balašević. On my brother's way out of
the bathroom, over my earphones I could hear him grumbling
about Chetnik music, though he wasn't saying it directly to me,
so to him, without taking the earphones off and facing the wall,
I said, "I can tell the difference between music and politics, I'm
not dense." He suddenly lunged at me and grabbed me by both
arms. He thrust his face into mine and shouted, "You don't get it,
do you!" There our conversation ended.

⊙ ⊙ ⊙

Pajamas, two pairs
Towels, two
Soap box, one
Toothbrush, one
Plastic cup, one
Slippers, one pair

The list was on a sheet of paper glued to the inside of the glass
doors to the girls' dorm. "Will you remember or should we write
it down?" asked Mama, rummaging through her handbag for a
pen. "I'll remember, I'm not senile," I said, peering inside. Those
were all the things I'd need once I moved into my dorm, my new
room. We'd signed me up, we'd had the conversation with the

head, there'd be no problems, plus I had a big advantage because I had no dad. I was a displaced person. I had no apartment. I was from Vukovar. Who could top that? While Mama talked in the office, I saw a few more girls in the halls. They didn't look especially interesting, they were scared and a little pitiful. The ones who usually lived here were not around, it was summer so they were home for vacation. But the stuff they'd put up on the doors announced their presence. They lived here and they were in charge. A poster of the Ramones on one door, heart-shaped and bear-shaped stickers, high heels snipped out of a magazine. Clearly there were all kinds. Who would be my roommates? We still didn't know. They'd give us our rooms on the first day when we moved in. Marina, Vesna, and Božana were assigned to a different dorm, across town, I had no idea which tram went there and I didn't know how to find out. I didn't know the street name or the number. I was assigned this one because it was closer to my new school. But not too close because I still had to take a tram and then walk. Mama and I went from the school to the dorm only once and I wasn't sure I'd know how again, even Mama had to ask the driver where to get off. All of us were in different schools, the high school for tourism, the high school for commerce, the gymnasium. I chose the gymnasium because I'd had perfect grades so far and my brother had attended a gymnasium so I obviously had to, just to make him stop calling me stupid. "So what about the tourism high school? You'd learn languages, and later, if you want to study you can, but if you don't, you don't have to." No. The gymnasium. I won second place in a national competition organized by the Zagreb European Center. The assignment was to write an essay on the theme "We'll build a house of sunlight and children's smiles!"

Europe. Sunlight. Children's smiles. A house. Each of these a theme of mine, and I had something to say about them all. I had a fine grasp of pathos and words of many syllables, and I knew what was expected of me. An optimistic forward-looking gaze without naming the culprit directly responsible for my woeful history. This went over big with the grown-ups. At the urging of my Croatian teacher I wrote essays for every occasion and on any topic for the school magazine, always with reference to the life of displaced persons. People adored them, especially my teacher. So she offered me this opportunity as well, and the answer came a few weeks later. There it was, I'd placed second in the national competition. The first three winners were allowed to enroll directly in any secondary school and received two pounds of Cedevita orange-drink mix and the *Serbo-Croatian Dictionary of Differences*. Mama called Uncle Grgo. "Which is the best Zagreb gymnasium?" she asked. "The seventh, that's where my wife's daughter is starting," he said. "It's the elite school." I wasn't sure what that meant. "The seventh gymnasium, that's where you're going," said Mama brightly, but she looked a little sad. The school was close to the center of town, it was easy to get there from the main square. No matter where we were going we always started at the main square. This was a reflex left over from when we first explored the city. School registration was teeming. Some students were there without their parents; they probably lived nearby. While we stood in line to submit our paperwork, again I heard a woman say: "They are all excellent students, the elite." When it was our turn, Mama handed a teacher our papers. He leafed through them and set them aside. "You made the cut?" he asked. Mama was a little confused; she pointed to the papers. "In there is her certificate from a national competition, she came in second. They said she has the right to direct enrollment." The man sighed and picked the papers up again. "Why didn't you say so?" "But she's had only excellent grades, we live in displaced persons housing, my husband went missing in Vukovar . . ." "The results will be posted on the bulletin board in a week," he cut her off and glanced up to see who was next.

⊚ ⊚ ⊚

We were allotted Papa's pension payments retroactively. We'd had no income all this time except for Mama's salary at Uncle Grgo's and our displaced persons' allowance, that's exactly what it was called, an allowance, and now we were given all the back pay at once. The rights of the missing began to be treated, finally, as equal to the rights of the dead, Papa was granted the rank of warrant officer, and we were given his pension. And everything owed to us. Mama agreed with my brother that we needed a car, Granny chipped in, and my brother bought a car. The new green car was parked in front of the hotel where we could see it from the window and from that moment on we watched it constantly. Every day somebody would turn up who wanted my brother to take them for a spin around the hotel, and he didn't mind; the car was brand-new. Along with our television set— our first purchase while we were squatting—and a refrigerator, which we bought at a discount through the association, the new green car was our biggest purchase. We're so privileged. That's what everybody says. You get pension benefits, food and importation privileges, enrollment in schools and dorms, trips to the seashore, and hey, you aren't walking around in rags. We're displaced persons so we're supposed to look mangy and snotty for all time. Like we've always been like that, we were supposed to be grateful no matter what. Professional lottery players. We're so privileged. Željka and her mother were granted an apartment in Zagreb. We kissed and hugged, the apartment was old but the ministry would renovate it, an apartment had turned up with the right square footage for the two of them and as soon as it was fixed up they'd go. We were happy but also sort of sad, we'd part ways for the first time in all these years. Željka's mother made stuffed peppers on her hot plate and had us over for dinner. They were happy, that much was obvious, but they said nothing about the apartment and I knew why, they didn't want us to feel worse, we, too, had been promised, after all, but would have longer to wait. I don't like meat much, but I ate and reached for more, it was so delicious and reminded my of my childhood, and my brother told me I was getting fat. Soon he left with the car keys, he didn't say where, he just up and left. In these rooms of ours there was no dining table, all we had was a desk against the wall and a little coffee table in the middle of the room. My mother and Željka's sat on the beds and ate, leaning over the low table: "How can a person's stomach not hurt when we have to eat bent over like this," said Željka's mother, and in her eyes I see a table, a high oak table with four chairs, in the new apartment. I sat on the floor and ate because I didn't fit on the bed, Željka was bent over me, my head rested on her knees and she ran her fingers through my hair. She used to do that when I was little and I'd just shut my eyes with pleasure, she was so tender and beautiful, the sister I never had. "Your turn is next, for sure," said the two of them, as if apologizing. "And before that you'll come for a sleepover at my place," laughed Željka and fixed my hair in a ponytail. She got up and went to do her makeup, she was going out with a boy, I don't love her as much as I used to, we're no longer equals and we won't be, she's the one with all the luck. Our mothers smoked cigarette after cigarette, exchanged tearful looks, and I went off to our room. Maybe Igor would call, he hadn't been in touch. My brother was still there, he was getting ready to go out; when I asked him where he was going, he just growled, "Tell Mama I'll sleep in the car." The night before he hadn't come home, Mama died of fright and since she knew he had a girlfriend at the hotel on the hill, she sent me in the morning to fetch him. This made me uncomfortable, him even more so, and now he was less dear to me. His girlfriend was everything to him and he had no time left for us. Igor was everything to me, too, but we couldn't see each other often because he lived elsewhere. We had coffee once and once we went to the movies. This was the first time after so many years that I'd been to the movies. We horsed around over coffee, he talked about his band that played in his garage and how they'd glued egg crates all over the walls. Then I started talking about music and he interrupted and starting kissing me and then we were mostly kissing. At the cinema we saw a movie about a pet detective, it was all they were showing, but mostly we were kissing and cuddling. On the way back we sat on the back seat of the bus and he quickly put his head in my lap. I ran my fingers through his hair and couldn't believe how cute he was. He tucked his hand under his head, and then he slipped it between my legs. I could hardly wait to get back to the hotel, I felt hot and uncomfortable and my leg hurt, I was so tense. He saw me off but never came inside, not even to the front desk. "So do you have your own room or live with your folks?" "I live with my old lady." This was my first time calling Mama my old lady, though I remembered, while we were still living in Vukovar, how I'd sworn I'd never refer to my parents as my "old folks," and I'd never smoke or wear torn pants. "My old man's missing," again, like somebody else was talking while I stood on the sidelines. I hadn't told him that before, it hadn't fit in anywhere. "Missing?" of course he had to ask, people who don't know us always ask. People from Zagorje, the kids, the foreigners, the morons. "Missing. He went missing in the war." "Ah, I see," he finally understood. Then he kissed me and said he'd be in touch. I'm still waiting.

◎ ◎ ◎

Each time I came in and turned on the light in our bathroom at the hotel, blackness scuttled over the sink edge, into the plumbing, every which way around the shower stall. In a second they'd vanish, I could only nab one or two, usually the plumper ones, the older trophy specimens trundling more slowly. At first I shrieked at night, the sight of them terrified me, they revolted us so much that we armed ourselves with a thick bludgeon of rolled-up newspapers to kill them, but then, as always, coexistence took over. Fast-forward a few years and we no longer even noticed them, and if we were bothered by one of them in the bathroom, all we needed was a thin sheet of toilet paper to squish it with our fingers. At one point, my brother even trapped a middle-aged one, judging by its size, in an old toothbrush case and called it Stevo. Stevo lived for a few weeks as our household pet. Mama was appalled but I found it hilarious. Cockroaches were around long before we were, and as things stand, they'll outlive us. Their survival depends on nothing and as time passes, the same holds true for us. We've survived. I got up for the fourth time, I was going to pee, probably nerves, I'll be off in the morning, I'm moving away to live among people I don't know. How long? Don't know. Alone. Mama's breathing soundlessly, maybe she's dead, maybe gone, maybe thinking.

How will things be when I go? When she's alone? A few weeks after me my brother will leave. What will happen to us? We're still kids, her kids, and we're everything she has, all that's left. She lives for us. I know she loves us but I cannot understand, she doesn't seem to be moving forward, it's like she's gone numb and is bracing herself to see what the next bad thing will be. Last week when we were in Zagreb she outfitted me with new clothes for the start of the school year, we had a nice time. We went into all the stores where we thought we might like something and I tried on everything that caught my eye. We giggled. Most of the time we didn't like the same things, I didn't want girly stuff with bright designs, I preferred things long, big, and brown. Except for a short lilac-colored coat. It was narrow, tailored of lilac wool, with a high-cut waist and little pockets. Wearing it, I looked like a character from a Dickens novel and I thought that was cool. Mama liked it, too. "It looks nice on you," she said, checking it out and smiling. She looked me in the eye, and in hers there were thousands more things to see. "I had one like it, well pretty much, dark blue. That's the kind of coat we wore when I was a girl, I was sixteen. I'm wearing it in a photograph with your papa, he's in a shearling coat made of real leather. Coats used to be warmer," she said while she stood behind me and watched us in the big store mirror.

She's as tall as I am, pretty soon I'll be taller, we aren't similar at all, she has dark skin and curly hair while my skin is pale, translucent, and my hair is straight, ash blond. They'll say I stole you, found you in a cabbage patch, that's what she used to tell me when I was small while she laughed and tickled me. When she went to work, I'd wait a few minutes for the bus to pull away and then I'd open her wardrobe and inspect her clothes on the hangers. I never took anything off or moved it, I'd just push my nose in among the dresses and inhale the scents of perfume from parties, dances, movies. I wanted to commit everything to memory, I'll have dresses like that, one day, when I have a husband, I'll have a red silk dress with polka dots to twirl in and I'll wear it when I dance all night. In my short yellow terry-cloth dress with spaghetti straps I'll go for coffee at the neighbor's and then we'll talk the night away; have you heard what happened, can you believe her husband left her, have you heard her sister died, have you heard he was fired, and all those fine and ordinary things. Meanwhile my daughter will curl up by my feet and pretend to be playing. That's how I pictured it, and I remember that coat of hers, not the actual coat, but from photographs. Whenever I went to stay with Nana for a few days, the visit would always start with Nana showing me Mama's wedding dress, and then when I'd had enough of posing in front of the mirror with the veil on, I'd drag out all the boxes with photographs and go through them. I always looked for Mama. The smallest Mama there was five, the picture was black and white, and she was frowning in a new hand-sewn dress with a floral design, standing by a fence and squinting at the sun. Behind her leaned a bicycle with huge wheels, and she got her first spanking because of it. They'd taken it without asking, she and her cousin who was two years older, and they planned to ride it down the only hill in the village. Her cousin was pumping the pedals and Mama riding sidesaddle and it didn't take them long to career into a mud puddle and bend the wheel out of shape on the bike Granddad used to go to work. When Granddad caught her, he spanked her so hard he, too, was crying. Nana told me all about it, her eyes full of tears, and I promised myself I'd pay him back one day when I grew up. Mama in a big city, in Belgrade, with a broad grin and big front teeth—her grown-up teeth had just come in—wearing a slim leotard, I picked her out among dozens of little girls. It was a jamboree held to celebrate Tito's birthday, *Happy birthday, little white violet*. A Mama a few years older was in the one I remember best, maybe because she looked not at all like herself but like a distant, thrilling, dangerous person, someone I didn't know. Mama's standing on a hillside, feet planted firmly apart, wearing flared trousers or, as she called them when she laughed at herself, bell-bottoms, and a black turtleneck. Her thick curls fall halfway down her back, and photographed from the side she looks feminine and attractive, but none of this interests her because she's taking aim, as if she's been doing it all her life. This is what a girl with a rifle looks like. A warrior woman from another world. Princess Leia. The gun was an air rifle, actually, and my mother was in the ninth grade and had joined the shooting team; Dragica, her best friend, was on the team, too, because of a boy named Tomo. In the next photograph my mother exudes self-awareness. In an incredibly short red skirt— which in the black-and-white photo was just a shade of gray but I knew it was red because I'd asked a thousand times—she stands between her friends Dragica and Željka. She's laughing, with one hand behind her back, probably hiding a cigarette, she's wearing knee-high boots with super thick soles, even though it's warm out. I know it is because behind them I see the Borovo swimming pool where dance parties were held. The girls in the picture are laughing because they'd fled the bus when the driver asked them for their tickets; they said they didn't have the change and with peals of laughter leaped out at the Borovo stop. That's where she met the cutest, coolest boy, whose brother worked in Germany, and when Mama asked him for a smoke he offered her Kents. He saw her home that night but only to her corner, my granny was waiting at the gate. He made a date and then didn't show. After that Mama wouldn't hear of him, but he came stubbornly every day to her school and her student job, until she finally agreed to go out with him again. Mama in her short dark-blue wool coat with the high waist at the snowy train station in Vinkovci with her arm through the arm of the young man in the shearling coat made of real leather, the train already at the station. There is something written on the train car in Cyrillic, I can't tell what, but I know the train is headed for Macedonia because that's where Papa served for a year in the army, they didn't make any promises but when he came back they picked up where they'd left off, at that snowy train station in Vinkovci. Nana and Granddad, totally different looking, Mama a few months older than she was in the earlier one, awash in the gleaming sun that had overexposed a part of the picture, Mama in a short silken Sunday dress with a bow on her ponytail, standing somewhere outdoors in nature abuzz with bugs, and behind her, a bronze sculpture, the sculpture of Josip Broz Tito that stands in front of his birthplace. Nana, Granddad, and Mama on an excursion to Kumrovec. Soon comes my favorite. Mama in a wedding dress, next to a friend in a formal gown, beside a big potted plant in the office of the justice of the peace, next to Papa wearing a suit. After the ceremony, they're smiling, a little differently now, shy, like everything changed after the night at Granny and Grandpa's house, her first night outside her own room not counting the times she spent at the seashore. Different after Granny's words: "You know he has nothing to offer but his ten fingers and you know what to expect from us." This was the next to last photograph that lived in Nana's box and belonged to the girl, not the wife of the young man in the picture. One more had found its way here, Mama must have given it to Nana when my brother was born. Looking tired, she's cradling a bundle and she herself is wrapped in a thick brown vest, because only one room was heated, her hair cut short while Granny stands in the background, her head sliced off by the picture. I can still hear Granny saying: "Your hair was the prettiest thing you had and now you've gone and cut it off."

All the rest I remember myself. No one believes me, but I remember the playpen they kept me in when I was a baby, the orange rim, the net with yellow and orange dots. It stood in the middle of the living room, in the morning it swam in sunshine, and Mama was tall, beautiful, and lively, she danced around me, she'd step away only sometimes into the kitchen. To cook or, as I later learned, to perch on the garbage can and hide from me a little. As long as I couldn't see her I'd play on my own; when I spotted her I'd reach out my arms. The linden trees smell nice, Mama's taking me for a walk, I'm wearing a velvety blue dress, everybody's greeting us on the street and admiring me, and Mama enjoys it and swells with pride. She takes me to see Auntie Tanja on Boris Kidrič Street, full of gracious old villas, so Auntie T. can sew me another dress and Mama can have coffee with her daughter, Milica. I stand on the table for them to measure me, I'm so small, maybe three, I remember it all, nobody believes me, then I raise my arms, I dance and twirl, and they clap, enchanted. Mama and I go to the open market Saturday mornings, Mama has a big basket and high-heeled sandals, I have a little red plastic basket and red clogs that I clack with like they're heels. At the market we buy everything we need, and the ladies tuck all sorts of treats into my basket, two chili peppers, an egg, two apples, and on and on. I know everything's for me. Mama sits at the dining room table and sobs. I'm scared, I don't know what this means, I've never heard grown-ups cry, especially not in front of kids. When she sees me she flashes a smile as if she's sheepish, but I can never get that image out of my mind. Mama's first tears. Granddad got drunk and wanted to kill himself, Nana asked Mama and Papa to come, she was at her wit's end. At the dining room table Mama kisses me on the head, my face is facing hers and she looks me squarely in the eye and says: "Today is a big day." I'm starting school. I'm only six, the youngest in my class, but I'm smart and big because Mama says I am. Mama and Papa in bed, I'm spying on them from the hall, a few days before we'll leave for the coast they're arguing quietly, I can hear bits: Why are you so stubborn? Don't you care about us? Damn *him* to hell, my kids are never going to be ashamed of me. I go to my room, afterward I sneak back, Mama's bare shoulder is sticking out from under the white sheet and she's sleeping in Papa's arms.

It's already daybreak, the mornings run one into the next, I look at Uncle Grgo's green bag under my bed. Mama has already had her second coffee, Željka's mother knocks softly at the door, I get out of bed, and Mama says, "No rush, there's time, your brother will drive you."

I'm moving to the dorm.

◉ ◉ ◉

They're still here, hanging around the entrance, Mama and my brother. He went out just now to check whether the car is still where he left it, parked across the street from the dorm where there're plenty of spaces, it's Sunday. Mama stands by the door, keeping an eye on my bag, I don't want them to go, but I also can hardly wait for them to leave so I don't have to see them anymore. I'm standing in line to report, there are a dozen girls in front of me, I have my documents in hand and I'm waiting to find out who my roommates will be. Suddenly someone peers over my shoulder and I hear a voice asking, "So you, too, have a displaced persons' ID?" Watching me with big, smiling eyes is a girl, a little older than me, and I feel as if I'm abroad and somebody who knows my language has spoken to me. "Yes, I do. Where are you from?" I ask right away, I see the familiar booklet in her hand, we quickly understand each other. "Vukovar," she says with our accent. "Me, too," I say, pleased, we don't know each other from before, but now we're here, we each have a displaced persons' ID, the displaced persons' allowance, a cozy room waiting for us somewhere in displaced persons' housing, and that's what matters. Now, in a lighter mood, I chat with the other girls and after I'm given my key I learn I'm sharing my room with a girl who's already finished high school, another who is new so nobody knows her yet, and a girl named Ivana, the most challenging girl on the floor, everybody avoids her and she doesn't wash much. Mama sees me up to the room, carries my bag, I'm in number eleven, the last room on the floor right next to the TV room that serves as a study hall during the day. While we lived in Kumrovec I thought there was no way to move three beds into a room that size so I'd imagined the beds must have been there to start with, and they'd built the walls around the beds. Here they'd been even more stingy. The room was small and four beds had been shoved in, one next to the other with only narrow space to pass. By each bed was a one-door miniature cupboard, and there was a desk by the window. The balcony was littered with cigarette butts, and across from it a large, spreading tree. I came in first so I chose the bed by the window and set my bag down. Mama stood in the doorway, I heard her heart breaking and her fingers melting, squeezing the door handle, and I didn't say a word. She strove to strike a cheery note: "Hey, in five days we'll be seeing each other, and in no time you'll make lots of new friends." I didn't tell her I don't want new friends, I hate new friends, all the friends I have are new because they haven't had time to become old, I just hugged her and said, "I know, Mama." It was already late afternoon when I saw the green car turn and drive away, and in it—everything I knew, while boys began to gather around my dorm from the boys' dorm across the street to see the new girls.

The girl from Vukovar was Nataša, she'd graduated from high school and was living in a barracks near Sisak. They'd moved there not long ago from Vela Luka where she spent a few years housed in a hotel. She was sweet. We didn't have much in common except our life story and it bonded us from day one. A little like sisters, one older, one younger, who hang out together not because they're so interesting to each other but because they share the same parents so it makes sense to stick together. It was already ten when I was in my pajamas and in bed, wondering what would happen if Igor tried to call me and reached the porter's desk, and I didn't hear the PA system summoning me and why was it that no one could ever reach me except through a front desk or a porter, when, without a knock, Ivana walked in.

I'd heard a lot about her already, her story went like this. When she was born, somewhere in the rural backwater of Dalmatinska Zagora, her mother was sixteen and passed her off to her grandparents. Later, when her mom finished high school and met a new man, she had new kids and never brought Ivana to live with her. Ivana knew who her father was, too, because in a small town like that everybody knows everything, and her dad knew Ivana was his daughter but never, never did he even say hello to her. Her grandparents were nasty, mean, and strict, and when she finished fourth grade they sent her to a convent school in Zagreb where she stayed all year except during summer vacation. When she finished elementary school she somehow won the right to attend a normal high school, so that's how she ended up at the dorm. She was going to a high school for agriculture, she was thick, brash, a weirdo, and she smelled bad, too. She burst into the room and dropped onto the bed. When she saw that I was there, she sized me up coolly with her dark eyes, gazing more at the window behind me, and asked: "So who are you?" I got up in my pajamas and went over to her, introduced myself, and extended my hand. I also asked her, "Would you like some cookies?" Ivana looked at me like I was from outer space and then she laughed, "You're a baby, your skin's perfect, Baby, that's what I'll call you," took a cookie, and went out onto the balcony. "Come on, Baby, come out and have a smoke with me," I could hear her say outside. Out I went out in my pajamas into the brisk big-city night and inhaled deeply, so deeply that it stung me where it always stung, and I coughed. Ivana burst out laughing, "Damn you!" she whacked me on the back, she was weird, sure, but, I soon realized she was the best roommate I'd ever have.

The little clock we'd bought at the open market beeped at seven zero zero, and that was when I'd jump out of bed to make it to breakfast and then to the tram and to school. My first day. Today's a big day for you. That's what Mama said while she brushed my hair but that was years ago, now nobody said anything. Ivana said hey when I went to the bathroom. Hey, I said, I'm all alone, things aren't so bad, they're getting better, I can do as I please.

◎ ◎ ◎

The tram was late. School was a curved building with two symmetrical entrances, one on each side, so of course I entered the wrong one, and when I finally found the right place, it took me ages to find Room 1F. "Hello, sorry I'm late, the tram was late." "Heh, heh." Softly, perhaps, but still audibly, the Lanas and Bornas I'd gone to school with when I was a Vukofuck refugee were now smirking; they were from the town center. The tram here is normal transportation, it's always late, you're bumbling, you look stupid, sit down and shut up. "What can we expect tomorrow if you're late the first day?" squawked a squat, frumpy woman, my new homeroom teacher, I knew she'd say that, so predictable. I sat in the first row where there was a seat by a girl whose hair was dyed blue, I felt their eyes on my back. Easy target. Introductions with an emphasis on hobbies started from the back, and by the time they'd reached the second row, I'd heard that most of the girls had been on the *Zvjezdice* kids' talent show. "You, too? Amazing!!" Most of the boys skied or played tennis, and one even stabled his horse at the Hippodrome. Most of the kids lived in the center of town on Martićeva or Gajeva streets; here or there was a kid whose ambitious folks lived in an outlying town not far from the city, and then there was me. I'm from Vukovar, Zagreb, Kumrovec, Zagreb, and I live in a dorm. These were the magic words. I was instantly the dorm girl. At recess a posse of three came over and asked, "So, hey, does that mean you've got no parents?" No, I felt like saying, I came from outer space, they found me in a cabbage patch, are they so stupid they don't know everybody has parents? "I live in a dorm for high school students, not an orphanage," I smiled, I don't know why I smiled, I felt silly. A little light bulb flickered above their heads, though not too brightly, they'd heard what they'd come for, they turned and left. I looked around, today was a big day, surely among them there must be good kids, kids who don't own a horse, or have a perfect voice, or a perfect grade point average, or special skills and interests, hobbies, goals. A girl looked over at me, I knew who she was by her first and last name, Mama'd told me, but she didn't come over and I didn't go to her. Uncle Grgo's stepdaughter, she kept to the friends she knew from before, maybe I interested her, but there was already one doer of good deeds in her family, it wasn't up to her to look after me. I saw another girl, for the third recess she was listening to her Walkman, she didn't take the earphones out until the teacher came into the classroom, she was dressed all in black, sat alone, maybe it was time for me to move to a new seat. We explored each other gradually but from the start it was clear, it was something like love at first sight. Zrinka looked me right in the eye, she didn't ask me anything, she didn't flash an empty smile, but she had a cool sense of humor, and she always had two kunas for a salty roll. I felt better each day I sat next to her, she didn't speak but I knew she was waiting and she cared. There

THE HOTEL TITO

was room for me in her dark gaze, for the seven operations she'd
been through on her spine, for her nickname, Robot—she'd
worn an iron girdle in elementary school—for her folks who
didn't understand all the pain she'd suffered though she looked
like she didn't need anybody, she could handle things herself.
I held her hand, sometimes I even hugged her, and she looked
at me, half-serious, and said: "Why'd you go all sappy?," calling
me only by my surname, but she didn't pull away, withdraw her
hand. We ran into each other one day on the way to school, we
were amused, we walked and talked. The sun was lovely, it was
late September, we walked arm in arm, she told me soon she'd be
going through another operation, she hoped it would be the last,
and she wouldn't be back in school until the beginning of the
next semester. Suddenly before our eyes stretched the expanse
of the main square and we looked at each other in surprise, how
did we get here? I thought she knew a shortcut to school and
she was following me, our physics class had already begun fifteen minutes earlier. We walked into class, everybody gawked
at us, they thought we'd been playing hooky, who'd even try to
explain otherwise. After class the homeroom teacher called me
in to the teachers' lounge to lay out a plan. On Tuesdays I could
take a Hungarian class, on Fridays, Japanese. Clearly I had too
much time on my hands and too little supervision, a few more
obligations wouldn't hurt. Zrinka died laughing while I con-
jured for her the high tones of our (least) favorite teacher and
her reprimand. I chose Japanese. After that first outing, physics
became a thorn so we found the choice an easy one, we'd sacri-
fice yet another physics class, last period on Thursday. Though
I'd have been glad to skip history after the teacher called me to
the blackboard and joined the ranks of the morons who'd been

at this school for years. "So, you're from Vukovar?" He squinted at me with his beady, red-rimmed eyes. Everybody knew he drank. "I am," I answered loudly and was reminded of how I'd stood, frozen, at the board in math class in elementary school while the teacher, Maca, tried to put me at ease, tactfully, with the words, "Why so tense? I'm not a Chetnik with a knife." They probably had the impression that our worst nightmares were Chetniks with knives in their teeth, they thought that's what war was. They all had something to say on the subject. "Come now, erase the board," said the professor. "The sponge is there, or how do you say sponge where you're from? *Sundjer*?" He guffawed, tickled by his own joke, and salvoes of laughter rolled across the class as they repeated the exotic word. *Sundjer*. "And where do your parents live?" asked the solicitous professor, and when I said my dad was missing, he asked, "Missing where?" Well if I knew where, he wouldn't be missing, would he, I said to myself, but to him, I said, "Dunno," and then we moved on to discuss the arrival of the Croats and everything that followed, and my face was still burning and I'd have been happiest if I could have fled. He passed me with a D, and, all smug, saw it as an act of charity, like people always do. But there it was, we fled physics, the teacher wasn't half bad, she was strict, nothing personal, we'd make it up next time. Zrinka was leaving the next week, she wouldn't be able to go out, so we had to skip out during the school day for a farewell drink. I had all the time in the world, I was allowed to be out till ten and once she'd gone I'd figure out where Marina's and Vesna's dorm was and go there after school. That was my plan. Hers was to come back after Christmas, and until then to survive and enjoy the morphine. We giggled and drank to that.

⊚ ⊚ ⊚

It was so strange, on the weekends, coming back to the hotel.
I felt like I was coming home, almost. Every year more of us were
going off to board in student housing, and then on Friday the
whole horde of us came trooping back, and the little old ladies
clustered around the front desk, done up in black kerchiefs
like birds on a telephone wire, and oversaw our noisy arrival.
Mama was up in our room, waiting to launder two bags of dirty
clothes by hand, my brother would get in tomorrow morning.
Kids chased each other around the halls, the drunks perched at
the bar, it was early yet, they had a strenuous night of it ahead,
lots of time had passed and there was more to come. Grandparents died, younger people also died sometimes, the village
cemetery was getting crowded. New children were born and no
one would ever be able to erase the fact that they were native to
Kumrovec, their numbers made up for the ones who'd passed
on. Maybe somebody has forgotten about us here and who
knows how much longer this life will flow along, unchecked. It
was nice being home. "Whatever took you so long?" the barrage
began at the door, what can I say in my defense, my classes at
school were in the morning shift but I didn't feel like coming
earlier, I waited for the others so we could take the bus together.
"But I've been waiting, I wait for you all week. Almost every day
I go to my job and then come back to this room, alone. Alone I
go to bed, alone I wake up and I'm always thinking of you two,
how you're doing and when you'll come." I understood her, I
felt that way, too, at first. Then I got to know people and places,
and I liked the ones I didn't know yet even more, I was glad to
be on my own in Zagreb. "Well, the homeroom teacher signed

me up for Japanese so I wouldn't have too much time on my hands, and the class is Friday afternoons, so I can't catch the three o'clock bus." "What right has she to sign you up, like you've no obligations and no family?" Mama was miffed. "That's what she thinks, I guess," I said in a conciliatory tone, I was starting to bullshit, it scared me and felt good. "Did you wash the sweater I left here last time?" This was a point of real interest, I wanted to go out tonight, Igor hadn't called in two weeks. He called the dorm only once, maybe ten days ago, but he wasn't at the disco last weekend. I didn't know what this meant or if we were still together, but I did know I had to be there tonight. "I did, yes, why?" "Well I thought I'd wear it tonight," I said, more softly. "Pardon? You're going out? Come on, really, can't you spend just one night at home?" She sounded disappointed, and then abruptly she stopped and said, "Go, go wherever you like, each of us lives our own life."

.I felt bad for her, I had an impulse to stay in the room but I went out anyway, something was driving me. We assembled at the front desk, by now that was the routine, we hadn't seen each other for five days so there was lots to catch up on. But they all roomed together at the dorm, Marina and her sister who'd begun taking us more seriously now, and Božana and Vesna, so they picked up where they left off, and I wasn't sure I always knew what was what. We went first for a drink at Kopitar, as we called the only café here, and then we went on to the Oaza. We were already regulars there. Tonight Dumbelina was there too, though we didn't call her that these days, we'd started treating her differently. She seldom went out, but ever since Tićo had dumped her, her sister and her sister's fiancé took her with them to get her out. Tićo and she had gotten engaged, too, but by the time I came back from the dorm, I heard the two of them weren't together anymore. He had hooked up with this older woman who had a son, and his mother and Nataša were frantic. Almost everybody was here, we ordered bamboos—our favorite cocktail—and Marina and her sister announced the drinks were on them tonight. We soon learned why. They were leaving. They'd been granted an apartment in Osijek and they were moving there after fall semester. We hugged and kissed, but it wasn't over yet. They wouldn't be leaving for another month but now we knew the day would come and there'd be fewer of us. Little Ivana had already left for Vinkovci, Jelena and her brother for Zagreb, and soon Željka and her mother were going, too. I tried to imagine what life would be like without them all, when we were left here alone. I finished off the last drops of my drink and said, "Let's go! Time's up!" It was maybe three hundred feet to the Oaza, but we staggered, sang, and stumbled, acting silly. My heart was pounding, like someone kicked me in the gut and knocked the air flat out of me.

I'd see him, very soon. It was crowded inside, too early for dancing so we ordered drinks and waited for things to pick up. Everything was smoky and dark but I saw fine, I fixated on every walking tangle about five feet ten inches tall, I was a live sensor for the long blond hair, the cute face, the lips my life was worth nothing without. There was no one who looked like that on the horizon, for the third time I went to the restroom, soon it would be midnight, there were more people, it was smokier, but my excitement ebbed, I was sadder. I went back to the dance floor, Ivan and Miro were sitting at the bar, drunk no doubt, but they no longer looked drunk even when they were, probably a question of training. "What's up, the high school kids don't hang around with us anymore?" quipped Miro, and I shot back, "Never did." They ordered me a bamboo, we clinked glasses. "You aren't still with that local clown are you?" Ivan asked me and, without waiting for an answer, he said, "It sucks when one of our girls hooks up with one of those blockheads. Why hang out with him? Is he a boy or a girl! Just look." I saw Ivan gazing off somewhere as he described him, and then I realized he was staring straight at Igor, who was standing by the door and chatting with a friend. I saw him, my heart pounded like crazy, he came after all, I was so glad. Looked like he'd spotted me but still he stood there, and then he came toward the bar and stopped two or three barstools away. Now I got it, he couldn't have missed seeing me, he didn't want to see me so I, too, pretended we didn't know each other anymore.

I'd had a feeling this might happen the whole time. There was no reason, I did nothing wrong, everything went like it was supposed to and then—it just fizzled. So predictable, like everything else in my life that had happened for no reason at all. Okay, the Serbs did their bit, but the real reason, tell me, is what? Ivan saw Igor and I weren't talking, and, beaming, he said: "Thank God you've ditched him, another bamboo to your health?" He grinned and I merely nodded, smiled, and drank it down to the dregs.

I need air, I have to go, I don't want to be here anymore, other people don't interest me, all I care about is going home and crawling into bed. Home, I think, is where Mama is. On the way to the door I have to pass him and I look at him, long and hard; he only glances over at me like we've never met, like just a few days ago he didn't have his hand in my shirt. The fresh air fills my lungs and at the same time it collides with something inside that wants out, nausea inches up my throat, but there it stays and chokes me.

I've never drunk this much, I've always played at being tipsy so I'd look cool, but this is the real thing. I barely stagger over to a bench and plunk down. I'd like to see how long this lasts, but I can't think, my head's spinning, if only I could throw up. I can't go up to the room like this, acid bubbles burning up in my throat, then down it goes, over and over, I don't know if you can die from this, probably not, but that's the way I feel. I sense somebody coming over, but I can't tell who, and when I think they're calling me a gush of vomit spews out and sprays all over my feet, the bench, my hair. I can't focus on what's happening around me, but I hear panicked shouts: "Geez, that's you! We've been looking for you for half an hour. You're drunk!" Like I don't know, is what I'd like to say to Marina, but I can't talk because I'm scared I'll throw up again, I just look at her. Finally I muster the strength to say, "I can't show up at my mother's like this." "Fucking shit, you sure are smashed," observes her sister. I nod, what smells so bad, oh that's my stinky hair. "Can you walk?" asks Marina. It will suffice to shake my head. The two of them consult and then her sister goes over to the phone booth. Marina rubs my back, standing as far away as she possibly can. I have been sitting for a whole century on this bench, Mama's going to kill me, but anyway my life is shit so who gives a shit. After a century and a half up pulls a white car, Marina's dad drives a car like that, and slowly (the thought takes twenty years to journey to my brain) I figure out that they called him to fetch us.

The first time in my life when I wanted to die of shame was when I threw dirt down from the balcony onto our neighbor Branka's head just for the fun of it, and she came up, walked right into the apartment, and caught me with a clump of dirt in my hand. Otherwise I was famous for good behavior and being super polite. Now this was the second time, but the wave of shame was worse. When he got out of the car, first he looked me over carefully and I sank my chin as low as it could go. Then he shook his head a little, sighed, and came over. He looked me in the eyes and said, "Come on now, take it slow, we'll have us a cup of coffee." That was the last thing I'd expected him to say, my legs wobbled and I was scared, but when he said that and even seemed to be smiling gently, I went limp. He grabbed me around the waist and I wrapped my arms around his neck, became him, let go, and forgot myself. He almost lifted me up, he was strong, my head slumped onto his shoulder. I am such a little girl, all I know is how to prattle and clutch Papa's hand. I feel tears, but who cares, I'm drunk, and when you're drunk you can do whatever you feel like doing. "It's okay," he says to me softly, thinking I'm crying for the shame, but that's not it now. I'm crying because it's my father holding me. Papa. "Papa, Papa, what did you bring me?" The car still hadn't pulled into the parking space in front of the building, but there it is, an olive-drab Yugo, brand-new. It's the prettiest car I've ever seen except Uncle's Mercedes. Papa gets out of the car, and I run into his arms and he hoists me up high, saying: "Who's my little scoundrel?" "Me, me, what've you got for your scoundrel?" I answer and ask quick. Papa always has loose change in his pocket that he earns in tips on the night shift as the maître d' at the hotel. "Here's for ice cream!" He tucks the coins into my hand, and I race back to the building where my friends are playing Chinese jump rope. Whose turn is it, rock paper scissors, and Papa slips up behind me, thrusts in his hand like he's offering a rock fist. The girls giggle, and then upstairs he goes, and, awed by his sparkle, Darija says, "You have such a super dad!" I'm proud the others can see.

Marina's dad starts the car and we pull out of the parking lot. Our car is brand-new. It's parked in the yard at Granny and Grandpa's house, we're washing it and I polish it with a chamois cloth. Only its lower sides, actually, because I'm still too small to reach all the way to the windows or roof. When we're done, Papa opens all the doors to let the car air out and I ask whether I can sit for a minute at the wheel and play. The hand brake is on, the keys have been removed from the ignition, so Papa lets me, when I ask him he lets me do everything. The grown-ups sit in the yard, they eat watermelon, my brother weaves in and out on his pony bike while I drive the car. I press all the buttons I can reach, I say rrmm, rrmm, and when I press one a little drawer pops open. Inside there are candies, no, pills, or maybe they're candies because they're small and pink, my favorite color. I know I'm not supposed to take pills, but I'll try just one, lick it, pills are always bitter, no one will notice. This one's sweet, not too sweet but not bitter either so I pop one after another into my mouth until the silver foil with little holes is empty. I could use it as a hotel for ants maybe, but I'm feeling a little dozy. A nap would be nice. Suddenly everybody's shouting, Papa's holding me in his arms like he does when we come home after we've been out visiting, except he keeps saying, "Don't go to sleep now, no sleeping!" I must've fallen asleep along the way, but we aren't home. Something smells weird like a hospital and then that's what it is, Papa isn't holding me anymore but I'm lying on a big bed on little wheels, they're pushing me on it, but he's here. His eyes are so big until he disappears behind white doors, and I hear a voice I don't know saying, "Now your tummy's going to hurt just a little." "That's not a little, I want my papa," I shout, he comes in. "Better if you're not here," I hear. "I wasn't where

I should've been," says Papa. My hand is small because Papa's two big hands wrap around it. Again I wake, now I'm already in my bed, Mama's cuddling me and saying, "You gave us quite the fright, don't you ever go doing that again. You ate Papa's pills for his sinuses and the doctors had to take them out of your tummy." "I thought they were candy. Do we still get to go to the beach?" I ask. "We do," says Mama, "you and Željka." My delight knows no bounds, not only because we're going swimming but because we'll all be going together. Seven of us pile into the Yugo. Željka and her mother, my mother and brother all sit in the backseat, my father drives, and Željka's dad—I called him Uncle Whiskers for his thick black mustache that moved at times all by itself or so it seemed to me—sits in the passenger seat up front. I was long convinced there was a little animal living under his nose, and if I came too close it might poke me. And besides, I had a huge crush on Uncle Whiskers. I sat in his lap in the car because I was the smallest, and if a policeman showed up on the road, I'd slither down and hide by his feet. That was one of the most thrilling parts of the ride to the beach. The other, when we finally set off, all loaded down like that, was that everybody would wait for me to start singing *Take you riding in my car, car, we'll be going far, far; come along with me, me, to the deep blue sea, sea!* and then they'd laugh, and I'd always sing it so I wouldn't forget how it went. Papa'd drive me to the ballet at the city theater, he'd drive me to visit to Granny, he'd drive me to the hotel when he had something quick to take care of and I'd be with him the whole time, he could take me anywhere. At the duty-free shop at the hotel he'd buy me a piece of chocolate or popcorn in a little sack, he'd say hi to everybody, shake hands with them all, they'd smile at me, and I'd play with the change-making machine, I'd run my fingers over the billiard table, imagine parties, dresses, dancing. The last week of school, Papa says, "If you bring home a certificate with an 'excellent' for comportment I'll take you out for a dish of ice cream as big as a house!" In my lap I clutch the sheet of paper with my name on it, I take care not to crumple it and wait for the waiter to bring it to me, four whole scoops. We sit on the terrace of the Hotel Danube, whoever walks by, Papa says, "She earned a certificate with an 'excellent' for comportment." I can smell the Danube there in front of us, the sun refracts through the water into all possible shades of green, soon the regatta will begin, this is the nicest place in the world. Papa takes me to the dentist. He's charming and handsome, he knows everybody and we never have to wait in line. He has little wrinkles around his eyes, that's how much he laughs. In the morning Mama makes breakfast, she gets us ready for school, work, the day, all in a rush and she's always hurrying. Papa takes the pot with the milk out of her hand and sets it on the table, then he grabs her by the hand like they're going to dance and Mama wriggles free, she's a little huffy, a little giggly, and says, "Come on, can't you see how much I still have to do." Off Papa goes to work, humming. He's mostly at work, Mama works too but she's at home more so when she says Papa will be taking us to school in the morning, we smile. Through my sleep I hear the alarm clock go off, but I can't get up, I'm so sleepy. Papa lifts me up from bed and carries me to the bathroom sink and splashes me with water. My brother gets himself up and when we're finally ready, off we go. It's winter so no wonder it's dark out, but only later do I see that nobody's out and about. Even odder, when we get to school the school's locked up, it's still dark inside, there isn't even a janitor around. Papa's confused, we look at him, and when he rolls back his sleeve to check his watch, he mutters through his teeth, "Oh, hell, damn damn damn!!!" We begin to figure out he wound his watch wrong and it's only ten to six. He looks at us, woeful, and says, "Nothing for it, home we go." We walk through the dark, I hold his hand and he smokes and blows puffs of smoke. At home I crawl back into bed all dressed but I can't fall asleep anymore because I feel so bad for Papa. I get up and go over to him, and he's sitting in the kitchen, drinking coffee. "It's going to be okay, Papa," I tell him because I think that's what you're supposed to say at times like this. Papa's face stretches into a broad grin, and he says, "Of course it will, Perka my sweet." I laugh, because when he calls me Perka I know everything will be fine. On Sundays Papa has to go to a drill for reservists. Mama's a little angry about it because he comes to dinner late, and a little tipsy. She and Željka's mother talk about this between themselves, because Uncle Whiskers is at the drill too. When he comes back he's always in a cheery mood, usually the two come back together and then they're silly and tell jokes. That part is fun, I try to memorize the jokes so I can tell them myself, because I know they'll laugh. The other day, when Uncle Grgo was here, I stood up on the chair, waved my arms around, and shouted, "No Albanian is going to be the boss in my house!" though I had no clue what it meant, or what Papa's joke meant that I later re-told: "What has a thousand teeth and two balls? A shark. And what has a thousand balls and two teeth? The City of Vukovar Defense Council. Ha ha ha!" They gasped with laughter and said, "One day you'll be an actress!"

Lots of things happened out in the yard at Granny's house. In the summer, when my uncle came, they'd eat and drink out there, make plans, live. "Come on," said Uncle, "stand there by the gate, we'll take our picture. One of just us men." They lined up, Grandpa, Uncle, Papa, and my brother, my aunt took the picture. I sat on the steps of the house and tapped the pavement with my new Puma sneakers, no one has sneakers like these, Papa brought them when he came back from Germany. My aunt turned around three times to glare at me, chilly and fierce, I was probably bugging her while she set up the Polaroid. This summer I saw one for the first time, where the picture pops right out of the camera, but I'd never ask, no way they'd let me hold it for a minute. The men were striking their pose, but my aunt suddenly turned to me and snapped: "Bitte!" I got all serious and felt my chin quiver, I hated that, but it always happened when someone shouted at me. I tried to catch Papa's eye and when I did, I saw him look over at me and he said, "Perka, come here!" I thought he'd scold me, I already knew I'd start to cry, but he just pulled me to him and said, "Stand here in front of me." He stroked my hair and exclaimed to the air, to no one in particular, "Well you sure can see by looking at her that she's one of us!" The camera clicked and there I am standing forever next to him, his hand shielding me, and me staring boldly at the woman behind the Polaroid, no one can touch me. The photograph was quickly ready and it moved to the front-hall table by the phone, and later it was put in a frame. There it stood until the moment when a Chetnik came into the house after he slit Grandpa's throat and said: "Hunt me down the others in this picture. All of them will end up like granddad here."

Now everything goes dark. I don't usually go there. I come to the brink, sniff the reek of death, stand for a minute or two, and run back. Tonight I'll do it, I'll go there and walk straight in and let it be the end of me. As I move closer I can already

hear the words: "Lie down! lie down!! Motherfucking Ustasha!"
He's somewhere in the middle, his face is in the mud. He's still
not afraid, he knows something is ending now, but he doesn't
yet sense what. Until tonight he was wearing a national guard
uniform and yellow boots, but now he's burned all his documents and donned a white coat like lots of others at the hospital
who aren't really wounded. The Red Cross will come. But the
ruse is pointless. Everybody knows him. He's the maître d' at
the hotel, he's on chatty terms with everybody, he's always there
when people sing, and if he can't be the loudest, he gives it his
level best, the veins bulge out on his neck. All his life he was
doing favors for everybody and they did favors for him, the man
with the most friends before, with the fewest friends now. He
loved people, but he loved Croatia, too, and when things began
unraveling, Granny and Grandpa fanned the flames. All the
provocative songs. And he did love to sing. Then the political
rallies, the new president, the quibbles over the Croatian flag.
This rubbed some people the wrong way, many were bothered
when they saw him walking, head held high, with his beautiful
wife through town and how everybody opened their doors for
him. But now it was their turn. The shaggy beasts. They saw it all
from their lairs, from below ground, and bided their time. Now
you'll pay! He lifted his face up from the mud and saw one of
his colleagues from work. He'd driven the man's wife, when she
went into labor, to the hospital in the middle of the night, and
now the man was standing by an officer, pretending not to know
him. Then he was smacked by a rifle butt and heard: "Lie down,
Ustasha trash!" He lay there for an age like that. It's cold on that
cold ground, but they don't feel it, they feel adrenaline, and now
a little fear as well. The drunken hordes of evil, snotty, ragtag

apparitions lurch around town on tanks, they sing *There will be meat galore, we'll be butchering Croats!*, they heave corpses into the Danube where they once bathed their hot-headed youth. These are bogeymen from hell, only partly human, they have hands, feet, and limbs, but with their hands, feet, and limbs they just butcher, slash, rape, no one can tell where they've come from, some look a little bit like neighbors who used to invite us to their saints' day parties. They leer with their rotten teeth, salute each other, gloat over mutilated bodies, guzzle brandy, there are women among them. How? How did they get here? It's slowly getting dark, the day is short, what a shame it's the last. People clamber out of the cellars, only half-alive, and with them are wan, sickly children, they're already on their way to the normal world, only a few miles away.

Now the time has come for the disposition of all of those who remain. There's a rumble in the distance, that's buses on their way. A camp is where they're headed. That's what he and Uncle Whiskers say to each other with their eyes, lying side by side, no one hears them. "Move it, swine, in you go!" A gauntlet forms of baseball bats, hoes, chains, rifle butts, and all objects capable of this alternate function. "Right this way, gentlemen, who'll go first?" They shield their heads with their arms, the blows rain down around them. An assortment of blows. Whacks, blows drawing blood, knocking the air out of the lungs, all kinds. Here's the mayor, to see to protocol. Some already collapse, not too many, these are done for, the others watch, horrified. No need, at least they're saved. Finally they're all packed in. Five buses pull away. It's difficult to see where they're headed in a night so thick with death. It makes no difference, around them everything's flat, crazy flat. They don't drive far, this isn't

Serbia, it looks familiar. The Ovčara industrial farm, a unit of the Vupik agricultural complex for husbandry and pig farming. There are big farm buildings here with large metal sliding doors for storing field equipment and tools and smaller doors for people as well. For small people, ordinary people, like you and me. They take them down from the buses and have them run the gauntlet again. Go, go, Jovo, give 'em the once-over! They organize them by building, bus by bus, but not everybody. No, no, not you. They pull out ten men, these'll be done by hand. Handiwork is always more valued, the assembly-line stuff is a breeze. A bullet to the brain, anybody can do that. But by hand, now for that you roll up your sleeves. You really dig in, put your heart in it, creativity, people will talk about it afterward. He's frightened. He cries. Tears run down his cheeks but he doesn't cry out loud, though what's the point of hiding it, and anyway no one can hear. Everybody's screaming so loudly, yelling for help, howling, the gunshots deafen. There are cameras here, too. Probably stolen, but that doesn't diminish the technological sophistication. "Motherfucking battery's dead, wait, Mile, for me to put in a fresh one." Mile stops what he's doing, drops his pistol to his side and waits for a new surge of energy so his glorious work can be captured for all time. "Done, shoot away!" Ten men stand in front of a building. The ten men think, let it be quick. One of them thinks of me. He thinks of Mama, my brother. Me again. There aren't any clear thoughts here, it's hard to maintain a flow, all the whooping, they smash, lop off fingers, shoot, stab, we're fine, we're in Zagreb, we're far away. They butcher. Handiwork. Done. Thank God. The one who's here to the end, he'll have it worst. Another nine hours of killing to go, hardly a walk in the park, he'll have to eat and drink something meanwhile, and maybe that will sustain him so he can be more effective. I'd like to think he was one of the first. But I know, what's in my head is an American movie, this is a fairy tale, a soap opera, never, never, no matter how hard I try will I be able to imagine it. And I'll try. My whole life I'll try. Amen.

Before I've even shut the door behind me, I'm greeted by an audible sigh. I know I'm irritating her by saying nothing, I make no excuses, I don't even fight. My brother's bed is made, she probably spent the whole evening by herself. All I want is to crawl under the blanket, fall asleep, and while I'm trying to do that her voice rouses me: "You must have had quite a night to be out so late. Hey, that's okay, go for it."

⊚ ⊚ ⊚

I hated Sunday. Lots of people hate Sunday, I know, but I hated it with every inch of my being. I spent the day waiting to go back to the dorm, I had to listen to how I'd come home the night before too late, did I need to review anything, and what kind of a school was this where there was no homework. Mama'd gone out somewhere, surprise surprise, probably to visit with Nana, and I saw my brother was getting ready to go out so I'd be getting up soon. My head throbbed, I didn't feel up to anything, and when I remembered I had a math test on Monday, I felt like flinging myself out the window. The rain began to fall, yet another autumn had begun, and in this dingy room the windows were at a tilt so you couldn't open them when it rained, because then the rain poured in, so you had to suffocate till it stopped. There was nobody in the halls, they were deserted, lots of people had already moved away, mostly it was old people still there. On the desk my brother left some letters, he probably took the clean copies to the mailbox and the drafts were left on the desk. One more stab. No hope.

October 30, 1996
MINISTRY OF DEFENSE OF THE REPUBLIC OF CROATIA
CROATIAN ARMY HEADQUARTERS
Deliver to: Chief Mr. Z. Č.

Dear Mr. Chief!
  I apologize for taking your precious time, but I find it necessary to write to you, because there are things I cannot understand so I'm asking you to find a little time and read this letter.
  I am the son of a Croatian defender who went missing at the Vukovar hospital in 1991. I won't write of the calvary that my sister, mother, and I have endured, but I simply wish to ask you to help us resolve our housing question.
  We submitted our petition for an apartment in 1991, and since then we have been given nothing but promises and lies, while apartments are granted to people with connections in high places. In regard to this I wrote a letter to the president's office a year ago. You sent a response to that letter which filled us with hope, but also disappointment because nobody ever paid any attention to our letter or tried to understand our problems. I am wondering whether the housing commission even wields any authority, because it's a fact that apartments are being given out right and left, and not according to a priority list or any other criteria.
  Today I petition you again, please help us resolve our housing question. My sister has started high school and thanks to her excellent grades she was able to enroll in the gymnasium directly,

but now she lives on her own in a dorm, far from our mother. I am a student but I have no conditions for studying, because we live in one little room that is only nine by nine feet.

I have tried to be as brief and clear as possible. I'm begging you to help us start leading a normal life, because I think we've earned that, since my grandfather, too, was killed in Vukovar as a member of the Croatian Army.

Thank you in advance.

Sincerely,

J. B.

Croatian Army Center p.p. 21

41295

I wonder whether he's writing this for himself, or Mama, or if he really thinks they're still reading our letters. If he does, maybe he shouldn't be accusing them of lying and giving away apartments as favors, because once they've read it we won't get anything. And the bit about his sister's excellent grades is a riot, I could die laughing. Despite her excellent grades his sister might flunk a few classes at the semester's end, though nobody knows this yet. Mama, who's no longer her confidante, doesn't know it, and certainly the folks from the housing commission don't. His sister might be reprimanded for skipping classes but this, too, they don't know, so what's next, oh, when the time comes I'll think about it. As it is we're living from one day to the next, that's what all people displaced like us say, so why would I be any different. Ever since Zrinka left I've no patience for sitting in class, especially some of the classes where they think of you as a lower life-form. Fine, there are some okay people. Like the Croatian teacher. The first assignment was brilliant, I aced it, I'm the best writer in class, obvious to everybody from day one. I never doubted it, but what good is that when it will never make you one of them, except when somebody needs you. A few days after the brilliant assignment a girl came to me with a request. "I have a favor to ask. My aunt died a few years ago and the anniversary of her death is coming up. Mama told me it would be nice for me to write something and send it to the newspaper, but I don't know what so I thought I'd ask if you could." "Sure," I said, I always say sure, that's probably the way I was raised, but I wonder who this crazy girl is. What am I to you, I never even met your aunt, doesn't that make you uncomfortable, but still.

Beloved Aunt,
The river of time flows quickly by and sweeps away with it our memories, but my heart will always be a sea into which all memories of you flow.
Love from your niece M.

On Monday her pals crowded around large-format newspaper pages and when they reached the Obituaries and Remembrances section, they patted their schoolmate on the back and smiled in sympathy. I only hope she doesn't faint, the freak. I haven't been to physics class for the second Thursday in a row, and seems I won't be making it to a third, there's a party on in the boys' dorm across the street. I'm hanging out with the crew from the dorm more now, at least there are different kinds of people there, but if I skip another class I could be in big trouble. I must come up with something; how can I avoid going to class without invoking doom. Terrifying how quickly I make up an excuse, how easy it is for me, how low I've fallen. So what, everyone else does it. I stand out in front of the teachers' lounge, it's recess, everybody's out in the yard except the teachers going in and out. "Could you please call my homeroom teacher?" I ask the bio prof who likes me, she nods and out comes my homeroom teacher. "What's up? Having a problem?" she says, sneering slightly, always expecting trouble from me, but never looking me in the eye. "Could you please release me from my last class, physics, today?" I ask, eyes to the floor. "See here, what do you think this is? A university? You come and go as you please? Where would you rather be this time?" The words tumble out in a rush, "There's a Mass for my dad. It starts at six." She finally clams up. What can she say. "Fine, go. Tell your mother to come see me." Oh sure I'll tell her, just like I told her about the meeting with my teachers two weeks ago, and when the homeroom teacher asked why she didn't come, I said Mama didn't have any bus connections from Kumrovec at that time of day. But I'll sort it all out sooner or later, I've got another month before the end of the semester. I always slip through somehow. I don't need much, once I put my mind to it everything hums along, I just have to sit myself down. If only I didn't have to see these people, either they pity me or I'm invisible. Monday I start being good, I swear. No more skipping classes. I leave the school, it's cold outside, November, but lively, it's always lively in Zagreb. I put on my earphones, Azra again, "A šta da radim kad odu prijatelji moji," this song is for me, it's my gift to myself. And what will I do? I'll walk to Borongaj, panhandle a kuna or two, watch people going places, light up a cigarette, the little match girl, get lost.

⊙ ⊙ ⊙

The parties at the boys' dorms are always the best. We tried a few times to hold one like theirs, but we never learned how they managed to come up with all the booze and cigarettes. The music was louder, the dark darker, and none of the dorm monitors would appear before midnight. "Come on, Baby, I'm waiting not a minute more," called Ivana from the hall, I put the last touches on my makeup which wasn't supposed to be visible and plaited my long braids, came out of the bathroom, my cameo in a lame Woodstock movie. Nana's dress was my favorite. Under it pants, red knee-high Docs, peace and marijuana symbols slung around my neck, everything smelling like a good time. Ivana had a flask in her pocket, I took a swig, but without a label saying what was in it I had no idea what I'd imbibed. Like I'm an expert on booze. I smiled when I remembered Mama: "Take care nobody spikes your drink." Maybe I would, if I knew what I was drinking. Ivana and I laughed, the party was near, just across the street, our worries were far away. The music was terrific. He was standing in the middle of the room and strumming wildly on an air guitar. He was older, definitely older, maybe even university-age, he was wicked handsome, and it didn't do to hang out with boys like that. Ivana sized up the situation. She knew me and saw he had long curly hair, black this time, a leather jacket, skinny pants. She looked, and then said, "He noticed you, too, Baby. Go ahead, join in." This went so easily, I took another swig and then over I went and started dancing near him. A slow song began soon and we put our arms around each other, pressed up close, his hair smelled nice but he didn't say anything so neither did I. After a few minutes, he whispered in my ear, "Should we go to my room." Something in my head said *no*. "Sure," I said. The room reeked. Six boys slept here, it wasn't as messy as it smelled.

Dirty socks, I guessed. I figured his was the bed with the guitar up against it. Yes, he was a senior, a student at the music high school, he was nineteen, actually, he'd missed a year when the war was at its worst in Bihać. I loved people who'd been through the war, right away they were more appealing and they could be as close to me as they liked. There was this understanding we had. And yes, his name was Dražen, he couldn't believe I was so young, I looked way older, he said while he sucked in smoke from some horribly smelly rolled cigarettes. My now quite *concrete* experience told me this could be weed, I just hoped he didn't get caught. When I told him at the dorm they called me Baby, he choked with laughter. We kissed. Dražen was on top of me. He undid my pants. He slipped his hand in, I could barely breathe, what do I do. "Come on, why so tense. All I'm doing is touching you and kissing you, do the same to me." I put my hand under his shirt and moved it up and down, I was embarrassed to touch any other part of him. I was no longer excited, I wanted to get him off me, I wanted to go, but I felt stupid saying anything. He started breathing faster, something was happening, I didn't know what, I still didn't know anything about all this, and then suddenly out of me burst, "Stop! Cut it out!" Dražen pulled away and said, "What's wrong, why the panic?" "Nothing, I just have to leave," I answered and did my pants up real quick. I was at the door when he shouted, "Where are you going? It's only just after midnight." This set an alarm jangling in my head, at midnight they locked the door to our dorm and I didn't know where I was, how to get out. I roamed around the dark halls and thought I'd cry, what was I thinking. Finally I found the stairs, hurtled down to the first floor and there I was on the street. Hurry, maybe the night guard hadn't gotten there yet, maybe he wouldn't lock up right away, maybe he knew there was a party. Maybe that was why they locked up. The door was barred. I couldn't believe it. Tears streamed down my face, I didn't make a sound but I was choking, I'd have to stay outside all night. If I rang they'd call Mama in the morning and tell her I didn't come in on time. If I stayed out there was a chance, a slim chance, they wouldn't notice I wasn't there. But where could I go, what would I do outdoors all night? Did I go back to the boys' dorm, the door was still open there. Maybe I could throw myself under a tram. Six hours, at least, I'd catch pneumonia. I was scared to go anywhere else, somebody might mug me, there were people in this city more desperate than me. Moron. I took off my backpack and set it on the concrete steps. I'd sit down here and wait. Survive the night. Somehow I'd manage. Survive the night. Six hours, then my cozy bed. I was in the afternoon shift, this thought warmed me like a ray of sunshine. And until then, hands tucked inside sleeves.

When I crawled into bed, everyone else was still sleeping. The blankets on the bed were rolled up and covered by a sheet, I bet Ivana did that, if the dorm matron made the rounds, she'd think I was in bed. When the monitor unlocked the door at six, I waited for him to go into his office where he smoked and then I slipped in. I still couldn't believe I'd squeaked by without being punished and that nobody caught on. If only I could warm my feet and stop shivering, that'd take about three days. It was so good to have a bed. I was shocked awake by the PA system, all sweaty I jumped up, I didn't know what time it was or whether I was late. The speakers were screaming my name, I had a phone call at the porter's desk, somewhere along the way I caught sight of an alarm clock, oh good, it was only 11:00. Groggy, I went down, the girl on duty came out of the booth where the phone was and with a smile handed me the receiver, even warning me: "Mama." "Hello?" I said. "Well how long does it take you to come down from your room, they've been calling you for five minutes over the loudspeakers, I hope you weren't asleep." No greeting, straight to the point. "Of course I wasn't, I was working on my math homework, but I wear earphones so other kids don't disturb my concentration." My brain, apparently, was still working. "How can you study with those things in your ears? Oh, forget it." Mama didn't wait for me to say a word, along she barreled. "Listen, your homeroom teacher called. She asked why I didn't come to the parents' evening and when would I come in. When were the teacher conferences?" A straightforward question. "Two weeks ago," a straightforward answer. "Why didn't you tell me, is something wrong?" One more. "Aw, nothing really, I just forgot, and then when I remembered it was too late, so what's the point?" I thought she knew I was lying and lying badly, I could do better. "I'm coming in tomorrow to talk with her, your brother's coming today after school. He'll wait for you out front." I said nothing. "Did you hear me?" she asked. "I did." "Bye," she said and didn't wait for me to say goodbye. This could be bad.

I took the tram twenty minutes early, I'd review the material before my first class, I'd offer to go to the board, raise my hand, make an effort, all the things I should have been doing, maybe the homeroom teacher would appreciate this and tomorrow wouldn't be a total train wreck. Until then all I had to do was survive my brother. I was guessing we'd fight. About what I didn't know, but we always did, maybe about: *You're not my father*. Just let him try to say something to me, I'd turn and leave. After six hours of torment I walked out of school. I didn't see anybody waiting for me, maybe he was late, maybe he wouldn't come. But across the street there was a boy standing in a jean jacket, in this cold weather who could that be but my brother who was ashamed to wear his puffy jacket because it was purple. He noticed me, too, we walked toward each other, but we were evading each other's eyes. "What's up, sis, amiga!" he greeted me in a breezy tone, he was always calling me weird names. "Not much, how about you?" What else could I ask him. "I'm fine, let's pick up the pace and catch the tram! Hustle, move it!" He grabbed me by the back of my neck and pushed me forward, then yanked me back, and then pushed me again. "Hey, slow down!" We laughed and acted silly, jumped onto the tram, and then I heard a familiar toot. I couldn't believe he'd farted in a tram full of people, and then he bugged his eyes out and started talking in this hoity-toity Zagreb accent. "You should be ashamed of yourself, young lady, I beg your pardon, but the smell is simply appalling!" I pounded him on the back and died laughing. When the euphoria let up, I asked him: "Where are we going?" "I'm taking you out for pizza, pudding, and chocolate milk, you can also get an apple and apple juice!" He reached into his pocket and pulled out a fan of colorful coupons. The student cafeteria was through the looking glass, my brother was the Easter Bunny, he piled dozens of items on my tray, asked what else I wanted, and then paid for it all with some change and we enjoyed the treat. I ate a whole pizza, a slice of cocoa cake, ice cream with pudding, a weird combination, and washed it all down with chocolate milk. My belly ached, but when I looked over at my backpack I saw a few more packets and almost threw up. My brother gorged himself, too, and in peace we sat quietly and enjoyed the clamor and rattle of cutlery. "She really needs to pull herself together," he said all of a sudden. Immediately I realized he was thinking of Mama, and I was grateful and happy he didn't mention my school, me, we could talk about her, anything, till tomorrow. I said what I thought she needed but he was already off onto something else, how she was angry at him when his roommate slipped him something. Candy? I didn't understand what sort of candy and how she knew, but I heard she showed up that day at his room and he barely managed to get up out of bed. "She's living in a world all her own," he said, I nodded, agreed, and he pushed something over the table into my fingers. I looked and saw a fifty-kuna bill and I leaned over to kiss him, and with a grimace of disgust he flinched. He'd had that gesture for ages, my brother, my big brother. "Mama's coming to school tomorrow," I said, but I couldn't tell the real truth even to him, there was no truth so valuable that I'd spoil what we were sharing this evening. We strolled slowly to my dorm, in the end I hugged him, I loved him so much. "Be smart, sis!" He looked at me sternly, and back in my room I said, "I was out with my brother." "You have a brother?" "Yes, an older brother." "You never said anything about him." My other roommate, Nikolina, was surprised. "Any pictures?" she asked. "Yes," I said and took out of my wallet a picture torn from his displaced person's ID. My brother didn't have one anymore. Once when he was fighting with Mama he'd torn it up and ever since he'd been buying his tram ticket instead of riding the trams for free because he didn't want to show it. "What business is it of theirs where I'm from." He'd also torn up his first student ID and sold us a story about how it fell into the Sava River, but they'd quickly made him a new one because he told the administration he'd lost it. After he'd left the room, Mama, tearstained, had gone into the bathroom and I'd picked the torn ID up off the floor, pulled out the little picture, and tucked it into my wallet. I carried with me pictures of everybody in our family, but at the time I still hadn't had one of him. "He's pretty cute," said Nikolina, "but he doesn't look like you." We don't look at all alike. He took after Mama, while I took after Papa. Seems we formed our attachments based on likeness, but sometimes I thought he hated Mama more than loved her. "Yes, he's handsome but he has a girlfriend, sorry," I smiled at Nikolina. His girlfriend was cool, the two of us hit it off, and if I ever heard anything about my brother, it was from her. Once I'd asked her, "Does he ever tell you anything, I mean about himself, about Papa, all that?" "Actually not often," she'd said, "when he fights with you two he's really sad, and when he's sad he doesn't say much, he just puts his head in my lap." "What does your brother do?" asked my roommate. "He's a law student," I said. "Well, well! A handsome attorney, if he splits up with his girlfriend let me know." "Sure!" I was certain he'd decided to study law, I even knew he'd passed two exams, but when he came home on the weekend I never saw him with books. I only saw him writing in his diary. He was always scribbling in that diary, and the notebooks with their leather covers were piled in his cupboard. When he was younger, he ran a piece of thread across the door of the cupboard so he'd see if someone touched his diaries, and ever since I'd noticed it, I'd never tried to open it, who knew what other traps he'd set. Once he'd left a diary on the table, but that had been ages ago. I'd read only the last two pages. On one page, with carefully shaded letters, he'd written "VukoWar" probably fifty times, and on the other page: "Dear God, please bring Papa back." At the end of the second page was written: "For two months I haven't written anything

in my diary, my miserable existence in a nutshell." At the time I
didn't understand what he meant, but now I, too, often used the
phrase "miserable existence" when I wrote in my diary.

◦ ◦ ◦

One of the eager beavers will know for sure. I must have seriously suppressed the information about when they schedule
conferences, and with it, the fact that the time would come
when I'd have to face the music about my plummeting grades,
the classes I'd skipped with no excuse and, God help me, the
ones I'd hustled an excuse for; the number was not small. "So
when are parent-teacher conferences?" I turned to the student
sitting behind me, she with the perfect average and, supposedly,
a modeling career for an agency in Zagreb. Oh, please. Modeling what? Hand cream? Her face didn't have much going for it.
"Tuesday after second period, and Wednesday after fifth. That's
for the afternoon shift. For the morning, it's only Tuesdays at the
end of the shift," she rattled and stopped right there. "Thank
you." Why be rude. I told Mama to come around 6:00, in other
words now, so she'll have to wait another hour, but maybe she'll
waylay the homeroom teacher before that. The bell for recess,
but I'd rather stay put, I might bump into her and I don't have
the courage to look her in the eye before the guillotine. Recess
lasts for ages and when the art teacher finally steps into class, I
breathe a sigh of relief, another forty-five minutes of life, use
them well. Blah, blah, blah, baptismal font this, baptismal font
that, not much of a subject so it's even harder for me to focus,
perhaps God is sending me a sign, though what the sign por-
tends I can't say. Someone knocks at the classroom door, in

comes the girl on duty. A bomb threat? A fire? Have the Serbs attacked us again? Any of these would do the trick. My least favorite option: she reads my name from a slip of paper, I'm being called to the teachers' lounge. This was to be expected, the class hums, whispers fly, theories spread. The two of them are standing in the lounge over an open book in which everything is written. Mama's face is stone, the homeroom teacher is pretending sympathy but I see she's gloating. "What's this?" asks Mama softly. "What's with the Thursdays? The grades?" The questions fire off at me, rhetorical, possibly, but I know I'll soon have to offer answers for all of them. And worst of all, and I hadn't pictured this, it's all happening in front of that dragon of a woman. She's tilted her head to the side and is waiting for my explanation. I say nothing. "Why aren't you talking?" asks Mama, with real sadness. Oof, this is where she gets me every time, I'd find a raging tantrum easier to bear. I still say nothing. "Look, know what," says the dragon, "I realize this isn't easy, Vukovar and all that stuff, but it's no breeze for others. A friend of mine's husband was run over by a tram at Maksimir, but her son is still an excellent student, and he's at the science and math school. Right?" I look at Mama and she seems to be catching on, "Excuse me? Vukovar and all that stuff?" she says slowly and turns to the homeroom teacher. "Well, you know, the war? Right? I know your dad's not around and all that, but dear child, pull yourself together or transfer out. Not every school is the right fit for every kid, and there are other good schools besides us. Well, now that we've had our little talk, if she decides to transfer, we'll let her pass the semester!" The homeroom teacher has laid out her proposal and she has this little smile, thinks she's given us a much more generous chance than what we'd expected, hope, salvation at the last moment. I know Mama, I know her well, she usually keeps quiet, but then there's a moment. I swear I see a bolt of lightning flash in her eyes and I sense something nasty is coming. "Excuse me!" her voice quavers. "You'll transfer my child to another school? What? Who are you, anyway! After everything we've been through, after everything my children have seen, you are going to decide this instead of me? She chose this school and she will graduate from it. She has her mother and do not think you can go around making plans for us. Summon the director, at once!" I am standing to the side, cheering for Mama. What I really want is to hug her, but it's wiser to stay at arm's length. Classroom doors open and teachers come out into the hall to hear what all the fuss is about. The homeroom teacher is insulted by the attack on her kind offer so she sneers: "And where will you go with grades like these?" Mama snaps back at her: "That's none of your business." She exits the director's office calm, serious but calm. "We're leaving now," she says and we leave. She walks quickly and says nothing, I follow her, three steps behind; I have no idea where we're going. We cross the street and to my surprise we go into a café right across from the school. She sits in the first booth and orders coffee with milk. "What would you like?" she asks and I, amazed, order a cola. She takes her cigarettes out of her handbag and lights one. "Do you smoke?" she asks me directly. This is not a moment for evasion; I opt for sincerity. "Now and then," I say softly, staring at the marble table. "Go on, then, have a smoke, don't lie to me and don't hide. You're better off smoking one with me than having a whole pack around the first corner." I light a cigarette and feel like a moron, and in my head I hear my brother's words: "dumped your pacifier and took up a cigarette, suits you like tits on a chicken." I brace myself and Mama starts. "Listen, I know you're having a rough time, but I will not countenance lies. It's not easy for me either, but you will not be giving up now. Hear me? You don't have to have perfect grades, but you will graduate from this school, if you transfer now you'll buckle every time you're faced with a challenge. Whenever a problem arises you'll surrender; face life straight on and do not run away. You're better than they are, hear me?" Mama is almost shouting, I believe it all and I look her cautiously in the eye to suggest she might speak more softly in this café crammed with high school students. "I could have given up, too, given up on everything. I could have divorced your dad when he brought me home to Granny and Grandpa where they could push me around, I could have thrown up my hands and let them send us off to an army barracks, or, God only knows, to an island, I could have sat there all day in our room and never fought for an apartment. I could've, but I didn't. I didn't because of you. And that's why you'll get through this school and you won't cave." She stops talking but her eyes are still eloquent. They're shimmering, flashing, they're telling me I can. We look at each other and smoke. "I want to go home with you," I say suddenly, my voice almost a sob, and I remember Alice nibbling the mushroom, if only I could shrink like that. Mama gazes at me with compassion. "Not now, you still have tomorrow and the next day at school, and then comes the weekend. If you want I'll come by on Friday and pick you up at the dorm, we'll go home together," says Mama tenderly, and the tears slide down my face, big fat tears, plopping onto the design on the tabletop. "Don't cry, hon," Mama holds my hand under the table, and this only makes me sadder still, that hand, if only it could soothe me till I fall asleep.

If only I didn't have to be alone in the dorm room, so alone when I lie down and close my eyes, like there's nobody left in the world. All I hear in the dark is my heart thumping like a rabbit's and sometimes I'm scared it will burn out or it won't be able to keep up and it'll stop. Sometimes I'm scared I'm no longer sane and everybody can tell. I'm scared I'll go crazy and I won't know what I'm doing and where I am, because no matter where I look, all I see are unfamiliar faces. How can I know there's anybody on my side, how can I expect that. "Listen," says Mama fiercely, "I went this morning to see General L., there were a few of us there from the Apel center, we went to talk about the rights of displaced persons, but I simply had to ask what was up with our apartment. And then something happened, something snapped, I couldn't bite my tongue. I started talking about how we're living, how we can't bear this anymore, I told him, imagine somebody sends your children to live in dorms after years of living in that room, how would you feel? I said all sorts of things, I'm telling you, the women just watched me, and when I finally stopped, Aunt Zdenka said to me, 'Hey, woman, do you know how to stop?' But I don't, I don't, and I can't do this anymore. Then he promised me yet again, as they always do, and I asked him, how can I know you'll keep your promise this time, I want something in writing. So he sent a fax to the housing commission and gave me a copy. I believe this time something will come of it, and then everything will be easier." "What will be easier?" I ask. I want to hear her say it. "You'll have your own room, you'll be able to listen to your cassette player as loud as you like, when you come home from school I'll make dinner, and every Sunday we'll bake cakes, you'll see, soon." It will happen, one day it will, I think, probably not soon, because Željka and her mother were granted their apartment a few months ago and still can't move in. I know all that, Mama knows it too, but we won't speak of it now. Still, I feel better, she feels better, we've sorted things out and now we can laugh a little about the homeroom teacher, Mama says, "Good God, what a lunatic." Soon we get up and we're leaving, and Mama sees me off to the tram, and says, "Keep it together!" "I will," I answer, just two more days, and, not counting today, just one.

◎ ◎ ◎

I was up at eight even though I was in the afternoon shift at school. I'd wound the alarm clock the night before after I made some decisions. I kept to the new rules all morning. By nine I was done with breakfast and tidying up, and then I went to study hall and after copying out the lyrics for "Like a Rolling Stone" in my diary I threw myself into studying. Suddenly, over the loudspeaker I heard my name, a phone call for me. Who could it be? I'd seen Mama the day before, my brother the day before that, but who cares, it was a welcome excuse for a break. I went down to the porter and when I leaned my ear to the receiver, I heard only a half sentence: "... apartment for us." "Pardon?" I said, and then I heard Mama, I heard words but I couldn't make sense of them or gather them into the sentence I'd been ready for almost half my life: "We've been granted an apartment!" *We got an apartment* shot through my head. Once more. *We got an apartment.* I wasn't sure I dared say it aloud. There were two sentences that lived somewhere in the sky, magical yet so familiar, because you'd said them over and over. One of them was *Papa's alive,* the other: *We got an apartment.* Now I should shriek, this was one of those moments, but I could barely muster the strength for my thin, little voice inquiring fearfully about the particulars. I managed to pull myself together and commit what she said to memory. The apartment was not in Zagreb but near, it was a two-bedroom in a new building, we could move in next week, but first, of course, we had to buy a few things so we'd have something to sleep on. Tomorrow we'd go see it, tomorrow was Saturday, it'd be a nice day, today we'd be given the keys, this had happened, truly, truly, I'm telling you. The girl who used to live in a dorm took off her sweats and got dressed for school, looked at herself in the mirror and couldn't wipe the grin from her face, couldn't wait for today to be over. Tomorrow began our new life. I'd believe it when I saw it.

⊚ ⊚ ⊚

We drove a long way. We'd left the city limits ages ago, but all I saw were family homes, like we were in a village, house after house, garden gates and front yards. Not an apartment building to be seen and I was already starting to think we were on the wrong road when suddenly in the distance glowed the red roofs of new buildings, taller than these houses. There they were. I hadn't seen such beautiful buildings in a long time, they were stylish, painted green, with arches and gables, so clean and bizarrely beautiful, cartoon-like. From the car I counted up to the fourth floor, in we went, there was an elevator. Apartment twenty-eight. Mama's hand shook when she took the keys from her handbag, two keys on a ring, one for the building entranceway, they called it a *haustor* like the Zagreb rock band, and the other for our apartment. She pushed the wrong key into the lock, in went the key but it wouldn't turn left or right. My brother said, "The other one, the other one." He yanked them out of Mama's hands and tried the other key. But the other wouldn't go in. Even a little. We stood by the door. We looked at each other. No one said a word. "Is ours a different one?" I said. "It says twenty-eight," both of them pounced on me. How long to stand there? Nobody else had moved into the building yet, there were no neighbors, we were just about to turn, and leave our apartment and the building behind. I supposed we shouldn't jimmy the lock again, that would be silly. We walked glumly to the elevator, but once we were downstairs we didn't know where to go. The only thing we heard were the voices of construction workers coming from corrugated tin sheds. My brother walked over, Mama called after him, "Where are you going, what can they do to help us?" He didn't answer and we trailed after him. He looked for the boss, a kindly man, my brother explained our predicament and the man didn't know whether he could help, but he'd certainly have a look at the drawings, maybe there were notes that would explain this. "Aha!" It was immediately clear to him while we looked on with impatience and waited for him to tell us the secret and hand us the joy we longed for. "You see, you were allotted apartment twenty-eight, but there's something crossed out here, it was switched with twenty-six. Our electrician has a daughter who requested an apartment in this building, and that's the one she liked best, so she took it. The other one is only a few square feet smaller, here, take a look." We were soaring, we had a place after all, this wasn't just a dream. What difference did it make, let the daughter take whichever one she wanted, as long as there was something left for us, we'd waited so long, we'd agree to anything. We'd agree to somebody snatching privileges that weren't theirs, we'd agree that we were just displaced persons anyway who were granted an apartment, so this smaller one was good enough for us, we'd agree that this was the way of the world, anything, just so we had a home. That we needn't have agreed and shouldn't have was clear to us only later.

◎ ◎ ◎

Whiteness. First I'm blinded by the unbelievable whiteness of the newly painted rooms. A clean room where no words have yet been spoken; the walls are virginal, there have been no quarrels here, nobody has sobbed in the bathroom, nobody has laughed. We examine room after room closely, walk gingerly on the parquet floor as if it isn't ours, discuss who will go where, but it all sounds like one of our fantasies, one day when we finally . . . "Here's your room," says Mama. I stare, incredulous; into the room I step and close the door behind me. Alone in my room. Here's where I'll bring my boyfriend. Here's where my friends will sleep over. That's where I'll put my cassette player. "Come on, we're leaving," knocks my brother. From now on everybody will have to knock. I'd stay here all day, but I have no reason to, there's no furniture yet, we've chosen everything and now we'll go back to our rooms to pack things in big black bags. Just as long as we leave the cockroaches behind—this thought obsesses us. No matter how much we inspect every single thing, blow into the bags to check for holes, we keep worrying they'll sneak in somewhere, or lay their eggs. Brown cockroaches. They're thought to be one of the oldest insect groups, fossilized remains have been found that are at least 200 million years old. They have survived to this day thanks to their unbelievable ability to adapt. They feed on human trash and food scraps and have a special penchant for sweet things. They also eat carrion. Meanwhile they transmit parasites and contaminate food. And they emit a stink that often lingers on the food and objects over which they scuttle. By day they hide in nooks and crevices and come out at night. Their flat, oval bodies allow them to squeeze through tiny openings in search of food or to flee from danger. The females lay their eggs and from them larvae are born and metamorphose to adulthood. Every single thing. Again and then once more for good luck.

◎ ◎ ◎

Now everything's a blur. All that matters is we're moving. When we buy things, it'll take time for them to be delivered, and until then we have so much to see to. Mama will quit her job at Uncle Grgo's. She announced this last week after we saw the apartment. Getting there wouldn't be easy, she'd have to take two buses and a tram. And besides, now we have more money than we did so her job, twice a week, is no longer essential. Mama will be dedicating herself to the apartment—she jokes that she's forgotten how to cook—and to us, to our new life. Recently Uncle Grgo has been drinking heavily, he always waits for her there after work and then sometimes he goes on and on about Papa, about the bandits, and sometimes he asks, "How have you managed on your own all these years? How can you bear it? Don't you miss having somebody with you besides the kids?" He usually starts in after a few whiskies and Mama invariably answers, "No one can take his place and nobody's going to tell my children how to live if their father can't." Or she says nothing at all. He tells her, "There are good men out there, you know." But there he stops and doesn't push it. He used to joke around, he always joked with me, but the last time I saw him he was solemn. I was on my way to school through the park. I hadn't seen him for at least a year, he was sitting on a bench, reading the paper; I recognized him straight away, "Well, hello, what brings you here?" He was glad and surprised I'd spotted him. "Hey, kid! My wife went in for a teacher conference and I'm waiting here. How's school?" "Okay, I guess," I said, I couldn't fudge it because his stepdaughter and I were classmates. "Don't you worry now. Things will sort themselves out, it takes time to settle in, school's a pain, I know. Your dad's nickname in school was Blade; you can imagine what he was like, he was the best." Grgo and I are friends, I've always thought so and I'm sorry I have to go; I'd like to sit and listen to him all day long. "Give my regards to your mother!" he called. That was the last time. And then, the shock. Mama called the office. First the phone rang and rang, and then Mladen, Uncle Grgo's colleague, picked up. Mama cheerfully reported our big news. He congratulated her. Silence. "What happened?" asked Mama. "Listen, I don't know how to break this to you but Grgo has killed himself." Mama sat down on the bed and went all small. "How?" she whispered. "Hanged himself. His sister found him. But, I dunno, none of us can believe it. Sure, he was drinking more lately and always talking about how he wasn't where he should've been, that he had no one left, that all his family are six feet under. But, you know, when a person drinks he talks shit. None of us thought ... The funeral's on Friday at Mirogoj ... Goodbye and, again, heartfelt congratulations." Mama started crying, she groaned aloud and we couldn't imagine what had happened. He was the only one who'd stood by us, kept alive another piece of Papa. One person less who'd loved him. His loss was the only thing that could distract us for a moment from the apartment.

⊙ ⊙ ⊙

His stepdaughter hasn't been at school the last couple of days. The teacher announced that her stepfather died and we should show her consideration when she came back. The sentiment almost sounded sincere but I know better, I bet she was advised to use those words. They say a person's died—as if it were from natural causes—even when he's killed himself. Nobody wants to have had anything to do with somebody who's killed himself, I get that, it means there's been a tragedy, a secret, like when somebody's missing, it's almost like others blame you for it. How nice it would be just to pass away. To contract a disease you can speak about above a whisper; others pity you but you die peacefully, you know why it's happening and how you're supposed to behave. The third day, when she came back, everybody hugged her, they asked her simple questions and spoke in soft voices. I went over to convey my condolences but she couldn't look me in the eye. She knew I knew and she was probably afraid I'd tell. During fourth period she suddenly bolted from the room; everybody understood why. I got up and went after her to the bathroom. Nobody understood why. I found her, crying. It was stupid now to hug her, but I wanted to say I was sorry. I wanted to say how I felt. I wanted to say that nobody in class would ever hear about it from me. Instead, I told her the worst lie of all: "I know it's rough for you now, but believe me, it gets easier." I could see she was moved and from that day forth she treated me differently. For a moment we had something in common.

◎ ◎ ◎

We chose the beds, we chose the kitchen cabinets, the din-
ing-room table, six chairs, a sectional sofa. We even chose a
still-life painting. All at one store. On it is a slice of watermelon
and a few apples, it's pretty and simple, pastels. These are the
kinds of paintings people have in their homes. We couldn't carry
most of it with us, they'd deliver it all soon, we left with only the
painting and one of those sleeper chairs, the mattress could be
folded up into an armchair, in case somebody needed to sleep
there before our things came. "Your brother will drop you off
in town so you don't have take the bus back to the dorm. We're
going to the hotel and I'll come to the apartment tomorrow to
wait for the table and chairs."

Not back to the dorm. I'll sleep the floor, that I can do, but
not the dorm. This will be my last night there. I've made up
my mind and nobody can sway me. I know Mama will have
fits, but what can she do about it; just a few weeks, she said, be
patient, but I can't bear it. Not now, not when we have our own
place, when I have my own room. I'll check out of the dorm
today. I've already packed all my things in two backpacks and
a plastic bag, I'm only worried about whether I'll know where
to get off the bus; I haven't gone there yet on my own. At the
dorm everybody knows I'm leaving, I've become so close to
some of the girls that I'm nearly crying and I promise they'll
come for a sleepover. One of the girls in the room next to mine
is a hairdresser and she promised me she'd dye my hair red for
free before I left. I've been thinking for ages about going red.
Ten of us convene in the bathroom. Somebody produces plastic
glasses, I've brought some bamboo cocktail mix, each will get a

sip; cigarettes and potato chips appear. The party moves to the white tiles and grungy showers. I prance around with a plastic bag on my head, I have no idea what Mama will do when she sees me, but that doesn't matter, a new life begins tomorrow. We giggle and clown and then orange-red water sluices down the drain, I haven't seen a thing but I hear gasps, wow, it's so red. I look up and see somebody else in the mirror, actually this is who I've always been, they agree, it looks fabulous. Only when I blow-dry my hair do I see how red I am, how green my eyes are, how pale my face. How broad my grin. I won't sleep tonight, I'll say goodbye to everybody and party, and tomorrow, tomorrow is beyond thinkable. Bright and early I'm already at the porter's desk. I fill out the form, de-register, the matron says they'll miss me after she asks what have I done to my hair. One backpack behind, another in front, a cap on my head. One more cigarette outdoors by the dorm with the weekend girls. Take care, dorm girls. The driver tells me I'm on the right bus, the trip will take about thirty minutes, he'll tell me where to get off. Some of the route is familiar, but when I get off the bus I'm not certain which way to go. I wander for a minute and then I see them, the buildings. The buildings form a single complex and our last name is already there, I know I'm home. Apartment twenty-six. I forget the elevator and panting I press the door handle, phew, unlocked, Mama's here. "Why are you here?" Mama is totally amazed. "I've come," I say. "Yes I see, but this is not what we discussed. Stay in the dorm for another few weeks." "I can't go back there," I say, calm. "Oh I know you want to move in as quickly as possible, but our things haven't come yet, so wait till we're ready." "I cannot go back," I repeat, enunciating to be clear. "What do you mean, you can't." "I de-registered." "Pardon? De-registered?

Now what? Where will you stay?" she asks like she still hasn't caught on. "Here," I answer and grin. "Oh, I could strangle you!" Mama relaxes and I realize this is the perfect moment to pull off my hat. "Christ!" shrieks Mama. "What now?" "I tinted my hair, how does it look?" I ask immediately, this is my only argument, it looks good, otherwise she'd have every right to douse me with bleach. "Heavens, could it be any redder? At least you could have warned me, I'm speechless . . ." The buzz of the unfamiliar doorbell. Saved by the table and six chairs. This is the most gorgeous moment of my new life.

◎ ◎ ◎

"Fuck you, life, I didn't sleep a wink," says my mother to Želj-ka's over the phone, and Željka's tells her she smoked a whole pack of cigarettes last night. She asks what she's up to, and Mama says, "Wall-staring." Their conversations in a nutshell. My brother usually emerges from his room at two in the afternoon, says nothing, and when he does speak, he says he's got to get out of here, he's going to Vukovar, he'll live there alone. He can't bear seeing her like this, not her, not me, I'm her spitting image. Recently we've been going to Vukovar more often, ever since the identifications began. Every weekend there's a funeral for somebody we used to know. Our turn hasn't come yet and it seems it won't. I get up at night, often I can't sleep. I've got to get out of here, too, as far away as possible, to a place where I won't feel like I'm going crazy. I might have a disease. Sometimes my heart misses a beat, my hands go numb, I can't breathe in deeply. I don't know, maybe Mama has cancer. Everybody's been getting cancer. Maybe my brother will be killed in a car accident and the two of us will be left alone. She'd never recover. She'd probably die. Maybe Papa's still alive. He's been gone ten years. It still happens. A woman from Vukovar was discovered by her daughter in Belgrade in a lunatic asylum. She didn't recognize her daughter anymore. It would be better not to come back at all.

Stop, stop it now! These are only thoughts, thoughts can't hurt. Breathe, breathe, in out. See, it's easy.

AFTERWORD

Ivana Bodrožić's autobiographical novel *The Hotel Tito* is one of the most powerful Croatian novels written about the war of the 1990s. It won the Zagreb Kiklop and the Banja Luka-Belgrade Kočićevo pero awards when it was published in 2010. The next year it appeared in a Serbian edition with Rende books in Belgrade, and has since been translated into Czech, Danish, French, German, Macedonian, Slovenian, and Turkish. Bodrožić also writes poetry and short stories, and her most recent novel, *The Hole*, was published in Zagreb in 2016. *The Hotel Tito*, called *Hotel Zagorje* in the original, describes the experience of the author's family. Bodrožić was born in the town of Vukovar, on the Croatian bank of the Danube River, on the border with Serbia. She and her brother were dispatched to an island on the Dalmatian coast during the summer of 1991 as hostilities began to intensify, and their mother joined them there while their father remained behind to defend Vukovar. That autumn, the Yugoslav People's Army besieged Vukovar for eighty-seven days, held off by fighters like the narrator's father. When the army broke the siege and the army and Serbian forces occupied the city, people came up out of the basements where they'd been sheltering from the shelling; women and children were allowed out and a few men managed to break through and escape, but the army took some four hundred men prisoner at the Vukovar hospital and bused them to the Ovčara farm on the outskirts, where soldiers and Serbian paramilitaries massacred the hostages over several days. Ivana Bodrožić's father was one of those who was captured and murdered; her experiences during the months and years that followed form the core of the novel. After fleeing the Vukovar war zone, the mother and two children in the novel are accommodated as displaced persons at a large conference center and hotel, known as the Political School, in the village of Kumrovec, the birthplace of Josip Broz Tito, president of Yugoslavia for forty years. Before the war the Political School and accompanying hotel facilities were frequently used for Communist Party meetings and other major conferences. For years the family share a single hotel room just large enough for their three beds, waiting to hear whether their father and husband has survived and when they'll be granted an apartment of their own.

Geography plays a key role in *The Hotel Tito*. Vukovar sits on the spot where the Vuka River flows into the Danube. The Danube forms the border between Croatia and Serbia, and it is many miles from Croatia's capital, Zagreb. When the children travel to the coast they traverse almost all of Croatia by bus. Then they move—first to Zagreb, in the center of Croatia, and, ultimately, to Kumrovec, just a short bus ride outside of Zagreb. Vukovar was far from Zagreb not only in miles, but in sympathy. The narrator is eloquent in her description of her sense of apartness as a displaced person. When the novel first came out it was read in Zagreb as a scathing indictment of the indifference manifested by Zagreb politicians, teachers, and schoolchildren to the plight of the Vukovar people. There was sympathy for a time, but the people of Vukovar were displaced from 1991 until 1997, when their city and the outlying areas were finally re-integrated into Croatia and many of them returned and rebuilt their homes. In the years after 1995, the limbo they were consigned to no longer concerned many of the people they interacted with on a daily basis.

REFERENCES

As the novel opens, the author sets the stage for the days leading up to the siege, as she and her brother are packing to go to an island off the coast with other Vukovar children. She makes a number of references, particularly in the opening paragraph, to the ominous political situation. To Croatian readers, particularly those of this generation, these references are far more accessible than they are likely to be to an American or English reader. The narrator, of course, is a nine-year-old child and she also doesn't understand everything she's hearing, but the fact that the details catch her attention suggests she has noticed their bite and weight, even if she doesn't understand them. Her father scolds her, for instance, for singing a song she's learned from her friends **Bora** (Bora is a Serbian boy's name) and Danijel. The song she's humming is a Serbian ditty boasting of territorial aspirations for a greater Serbia. The word *ćale* is Serbian slang for "dad" or "papa." Her father's irritation with her use of the word and her singing of the song, and his reference to **him** in "Damn **him** to hell" (meaning Slobodan Milošević, Serbia's president) is symptomatic of the tensions of the moment.

The mention of **Meso** the monkey (p. 8) is a reference to

Stipe Mesić, the last president of Yugoslavia (Jun 30, 1991, to December 6, 1991). Later, he also served as president of Croatia from 2000 to 2010.

Tajči (p. 9) was a Croatian pop singer in the late 1980s. She represented Yugoslavia at the 1990 Eurovision Song Contest when Zagreb was the host, and her song "Let's Go Crazy" came in seventh. Her signature hairdo was a cross between Olivia Newton-John's (as "bad" Sandy) in *Grease* and Marilyn Monroe's.

The song "**Moja Ružo**" (p. 13) by the Zagreb band Prljavo Kazalište became the anthem of loss during the first year of the war, hence the symbolism of playing it over the radio on the day the Vukovar siege was broken and the city occupied by Serbian forces and the Yugoslav People's Army. The lyrics describe the death of the songwriter's mother, Ruža (Rose); the refrain refers to her as "the last Rose of Croatia."

Elementary schools and high schools in Croatia run on two **shifts** (p. 26) one in the morning, running from 8:00 a.m. to 2:00 p.m., and the other in the afternoon, from 2:00 p.m. to 7:00 p.m. One week a child attends school in the morning shift, the next week in the afternoon shift, alternating weeks throughout the school year.

When the narrator doesn't understand everything during her conversation with her Italian father about the city of **Zadar** (p. 53), what she doesn't know is that before the Second World War, Zadar was an Italian city. Her Italian father's father, Giuseppe, was presumably an Italian fascist soldier who fought there during the war.

Kulen (p. 59) is a coveted traditional spicy smoked sausage, often homemade, typical for the cuisine of the region of Slavonia and the city of Vukovar.

Croatia's first president, Franjo Tudjman, replaced the Yugoslav word for "passport," pasoš, with the Croatian term **putovnica** (p. 62) as part of a sweeping language reform following the Croatian secession from Yugoslavia in 1991; the introduction of the word *putovnica* has come to symbolize the political and cultural transition from Communism.

The late-night TV show *Slikom na sliku* (p. 71) ran from 1991 to 1996 on Zagreb television, and offered a digest of war-related news. Because it often showed footage taken at the various fronts, people searching for missing loved ones watched it just in case they might spot a familiar face in the footage.

The **Intercontinental** (p. 94) was the most luxurious hotel in Zagreb when it first opened in the 1970s. During the war, displaced persons were housed in hotels all over Croatia, including the Intercontinental, now a part of the Westin hotel chain.

"**Bolje biti pijan nego star**" (p. 95) (Better to be drunk than old) is a line from a song by the Bosnian band Plavi Orkestar.

Djordje Balašević (p. 103) is a singer known for his folk-rock ballads. He enjoys a widespread following throughout Croatia, Serbia, Bosnia, and Montenegro. The narrator's brother mutters about **Chetnik** music because Balašević is a Serb. The **Chetniks** were a military group that backed the ousted Serbian king during the Second World War. The term continues to be used as a derogatory epithet for Serbs, particularly Serbian combatants.

The **Ustasha** were a fighting force constituted by the Independent State of Croatia, a Nazi puppet state, during the Second World War. The term continues to be used as a derogatory epithet for Croats, particularly Croatian combatants.

The *Serbo-Croatian Dictionary of Differences* (p. 105). The prize the narrator received was a volume published in 1991 describing the differences in vocabulary between the Serbian and Croatian languages.

The **quibbles over the Croatian flag** (p. 134) refer to a controversy from the summer of 1991, just a few months before the Vukovar siege began. The flag's design included a shield containing a red-and-white checkerboard symbol long used in Croatian insignia. During the Second World War, the checkerboard on the shield started first with a white square, followed by a red square. While some insisted on starting the checkerboard on the new flag with a red square, in order to distance the 1990s flag from that of 1940s fascism, others championed the "white square first." The checkerboard shield on Croatia's flag today begins with a red square.

"A šta da radim kad odu prijatelji moji" (p. 141) (And what will I do when my friends go away) is a line from a song by the band Azra.

Haustor (p. 155) was a popular Zagreb band in the 1970s and '80s. The word refers to the street entrance to an apartment building. The closest we have to it in United States cities is a back alley, the realm of trash cans and feral cats.

The **identifications** (p. 163) were the process of identifying the remains of bodies exhumed from various sites in and around Vukovar, including the site of the Ovčara massacre.

A note on the Vukovar atrocities: Three trials were held to address the Vukovar atrocities at the International Criminal Tribunal for the former Yugoslavia in The Hague (where I worked for six years) but none of these has satisfactorily plumbed what happened there. During the first Vukovar trial, the town's **mayor**—who makes a brief appearance in the novel (p. 135)—committed suicide while in the Hague prison before his verdict was read. The second was the trial of three Yugo-slav People's Army officers who organized the Ovčara massacre described in the novel, but many feel justice was not served: the trial was poorly run. The defendant in the third trial died of cancer before his trial could reach completion.

Ellen Elias-Bursać
Boston, January 2017

IVANA BODROŽIĆ was born in Vukovar in 1982 where she lived until the Yugoslav wars started in 1991 when she then moved to Kumrovec where she stayed with her family at a hotel for displaced persons. She studied at the Faculty of Humanities and Social Sciences in Zagreb. In 2005, she published her first poetry collection, entitled *Prvi korak u tamu* (*The First Step into Darkness*). Her first novel *Hotel Zagorje* (*The Hotel Tito*) was published in 2010, receiving high praise from both critics and audiences and becoming a Croatian bestseller. She has since published her second poetry collection *Prijelaz za divlje životinje* (*A Crossing for Wild Animals*) and a short story collection *100% pamuk* (100% Cotton), which has also won a regional award. Her most recent novel, the political thriller *Hole*, has sparked controversy and curiosity among Croatian readers.

ELLEN ELIAS-BURSAĆ is a translator of fiction and non-fiction from Bosnian, Croatian, and Serbian. Her translation of David Albahari's novel *Götz and Meyer* won the 2006 ALTA National Translation Award. She taught for ten years in the Harvard University Slavic Department, worked as a language reviser at the International Criminal Tribunal for the former Yugoslavia in The Hague, and is a contributing editor to the online journal *Asymptote*. Her book *Translating Evidence and Interpreting Testimony at a War Crimes Tribunal* was given the Mary Zirin Prize in 2015.

ABOUT SEVEN STORIES PRESS

Seven Stories Press is an independent book publisher based in New York City. We publish works of the imagination by such writers as Nelson Algren, Russell Banks, Octavia E. Butler, Ani DiFranco, Assia Djebar, Ariel Dorfman, Coco Fusco, Barry Gifford, Martha Long, Luis Negrón, Hwang Sok-yong, Lee Stringer, and Kurt Vonnegut, to name a few, together with political titles by voices of conscience, including Subhankar Banerjee, the Boston Women's Health Collective, Noam Chomsky, Angela Y. Davis, Human Rights Watch, Derrick Jensen, Ralph Nader, Loretta Napoleoni, Gary Null, Greg Palast, Project Censored, Barbara Seaman, Alice Walker, Gary Webb, and Howard Zinn, among many others. Seven Stories Press believes publishers have a special responsibility to defend free speech and human rights, and to celebrate the gifts of the human imagination, wherever we can. In 2012 we launched Triangle Square books for young readers with strong social justice and narrative components, telling personal stories of courage and commitment. For additional information, visit www.sevenstories.com.